SEA MONSTER TATTOO
AND OTHER STORIES

Sea Monster Tattoo
and other stories

Ruth Thomas

Polygon
Edinburgh

First published by
Polygon
22 George Square
Edinburgh

Set in Galliard by Palimpsest Book Production Limited,
Polmont, Stirlingshire
Printed and bound in Great Britain by
Cromwell Press, Broughton Gifford, Melksham, Wiltshire.

A CIP record is available for this title.

ISBN 0 7486 6226 X

The Publisher acknowledges subsidy from

THE SCOTTISH ARTS COUNCIL

towards the publication of this volume.

To Mike

Contents

Acknowledgements

I would like to thank my parents, Liz and Eric Thomas, for their enthusiasm from the beginning.

Thank you to the Scottish Arts Council Literature Department for its generous financial support, and to Marion Sinclair, Robert Alan Jamieson and the Polygon editorial team for their commitment. Many thanks also to the writers of Edinburgh's South Side, Gorgie Dalry and City Farm workshops, and to Jennie Renton, Sandie Craigie, Melissa Ross, Carol Graham, Alice Taylor, Olga Osipenko and my sister Ann Jones, for their encouragement.

And to the memory of our cat Bonzo.

Umbilical Oranges

I S IT FRESH?
   Are they ripe?
I need a tin opener/bucket/frying pan
Sometimes she takes the phrase book into shops so she can
ask for things. But it sounds hysterical after a while, it sounds
as if the happy holiday-maker has gone insane.
   In this city cars hoot at you all the time, and men shout out
of windows. They don't whistle the way they did in Edinburgh.
They just shout or sum you up in a mysterious sentence as they
walk past. Sometimes they say 'Si' under their breath. Men are
more in evidence on the streets. Women stay at home while men
flop in parks, soaking up the sun like big ugly water-lilies. There is
a kiddies' playground near the Institute, and old men with black
trilbies sit on the swings. Moira walks past them every day.
   Working at the Institute pays her rent and her ticket home.
It's a big, sanitary place with a picture of Big Ben and children
singing British nursery rhymes and it makes her nervous. Every so
often she has to run away to make herself a coffee with powdered
milk. The rest of the staff drink Maté: tea that tastes like boiled
pot pourri, that they suck through a metal straw. This evening
Moira has to talk to a new man called Señor Diez. She just has
to sit there for an hour and talk English. He wants to improve,
wants a quick Anglo-Saxon blast before a business trip. When
she arrives she can see him through the glass panels of the front
door. He is wearing a leather jacket. He has a face like a sheet

of fanfold paper, and small clean hands. The room smells of aftershave; it reminds her of failed relationships. 'Glad to meet you,' says Señor Diez, chewing gum, then he kisses Moira on the right cheek. Somehow he has an American accent; his words slur together, get mixed up with the gum.

Pleased to meet you. She is primly teacherish. They sit down and she rustles her bag around for a while, making a performance with her pens and books, banging notepaper square like a newsreader. She lies her watch on the table. It is three minutes past seven. She says —Well! – And her brain gropes like tendrils for something.

What do you do? What is it that you do?

In teaching courses, this would be called something like 'Breaking the Ice'. But all she can think of is the game where you pass oranges around with your chin. Señor Diez says, 'I am gynaecologist.'

Really?

Her voice is small, as if she's speaking down a paper telephone. His eyes are like empty beer kegs. She looks down at her notebook but it is empty, little fringes of paper clinging to the spirals. When she looks up there are oranges looming at the window. Naranjas Ombilicas. Umbilical oranges.

Woman is my life, says Señor Diez. I work with woman. I have wife and three daughters.

His eyes are like empty beer kegs. They seem to see her, see her quaking.

The streets in this city have numbers, not names. Moira counts them when she walks. 35, 36, 37. The Institute is on 38. Crossing the roads she always looks both ways because she distrusts herself. She has this instinct for turning her head in the wrong direction. Perhaps one day a bus might develop a British complex and appear when she least expects it. And here you have to look after yourself. Cars trample the streets like lunatic bulls, blasting and stinking of diesel. She starts off confidently, but sometimes gets transfixed in the middle, wondering which way to look.

La Plata.

Dear Miss Douglas, she wrote to her old landlady, Dear Miss Douglas. Well, here I am in La Plata and it feels very strange. It's about an hour and a half's drive from Buenos Aires . . . She never writes good postcards. They always slip away from what she means and end up sounding like guide books. La Plata: a medium-sized city, based on a grid system like New York, where streets have numbers, not names. She lives on 33rd Street. It is like living in a crossword puzzle. 33 across and 9 down. On 9th Street Moira always meets the same woman, who is always pouring water on the pavement. Little drops of water land on Moira's jeans. And she smiles, trying to show that she doesn't mind. She doesn't speak Spanish, but she is learning vocabulary from billboards.

Naranjas = Oranges. It's strange to look at oranges on trees, not in string bags. You can get them dirt cheap here, free if you pick them. There are two on either side of Señor Diez' head. He moves his head from one side to the other, so sometimes the oranges disappear and then bob back again. He talks about the weather.

—The summer here is very hot. You have beautiful tan when you live here.

Moira wonders if they are edible, the oranges on either side of his head. But perhaps street oranges are just ornamental, which is why nobody picks them. Perhaps they're just meant to sparkle away there, in the sun.

In Edinburgh it always rains and everyone is so sarcastic. 'Another lovely day!' Everyone says that, smiling, beneath raincoats. It rains so often that the sarcasm has almost been forgotten. The weather is always wet, everyone skulking around trying to avoid saturation. When she lived there she used to walk down Princes Street on her way home, and every time she went into department stores she saw stressed, wet reflections of herself. Edinburgh residents seeking solace in a bit of mundane shopping, a bar of soap, a bottle of TCP. Everyone gently steaming in the warmth, unzipping their anoraks. It had a foggy mountain atmosphere, a wet day in Boots. Then one day

3

a woman had hit Moira with a wet carrier bag. She had stood in the depilatories aisle and whacked her with a white bag that said KEEN COSTS. It was astonishing, that things could have got so bad. People had become so tired of the greyness that they were starting to hit each other in department stores. Moira opened her mouth and screamed. She screamed at the woman, who had lavender bath cubes in her trolley, and the woman seemed to shudder like a nervous animal and she trembled away into the toothpaste section. Shortly afterwards Moira had borrowed money and left the country. In Edinburgh everyone said, 'Your hands are like ice-cubes.' She was permanently mottled. Cold.

Now she was here and still thinking about the cold, Edinburgh's white sky dreichness. Maybe she was in love with it. Everyone sneezing over each other and warming their hands on the sulphurous lump of a wrapped fish supper. In Scotland now there would be root vegetables. A lot of parsnips in the shops, and turnips. People would be carving difficult, disfigured faces into them for lanterns, and they'd be rustling round the department stores with gold pre-Christmas bags, sneezing over each other, fighting over plates in the mid-season sales. In Edinburgh there'd be the brewing smell of hot stagnant Weetabix on freezing mornings, at bus stops. Also the smell of stale beer and warm air wheeching beneath pub doors at night, dragged out by the ventilation system. The fumes of warm drinkers.

Miss Douglas sent her a postcard.

—Dear Moira. La Plata sounds very geometrical. Edinburgh is still cold, it's still very difficult to cycle up the Mound. I wonder if you have been to the Pampas?—

Everyone asks about the Pampas but she has not been there yet. She has been to Buenos Aires on the coach, a long hot vehicle barging with broken headrests down the highway, not like the Lothian Region Transport buses that have adverts on the walls saying 'Visit the tulip fields of Holland'. But the passengers still look as if they're on their way to Leith. They recline their seats and go to sleep while Moira looks out of the window at the flat land and the shacks and the bony dogs and happy cows. The trees are sprayed white and

4

covered with statements of love and politics. In Edinburgh this happens in lifts.

Between the oranges, Señor Diez stares and tells Moira that he is going to a conference about the menopause. She does not know what to say. He sits very still, physiological with neat hands, and asks her what music she likes. The lesson is getting out of control, reversing itself. She hates questions. She can never think how to answer.

—And what like is Edinburgh? he says.

Edinburgh is a beautiful and old city. It is beautiful and old and full of theatres and museums and cinemas. Lots to do and see. She cannot remember for the moment what there is to do and see. He wants to know about the Castle and about clans. Do you have a clan? What is your tartan? She just has a picture in her mind of the sky in Edinburgh, of walking across North Bridge and looking at the sky. Pale grey with seagulls in it. A view of the Firth. It's raining. Have you been to Scotland? she says, flipping the questions the right way round.

—No. I don't like travel. I don't like to fly. That's my problem, says Señor Diez. – We say here, your country is your country. He blinks.

—Hmmmm, says Moira, trying to look thoughtful. Let me think of an equivalent. Perhaps . . .

Home Sweet Home? Haste Ye Back? I'm A Real Scot From Edinburgh?

—British girls are lonely, says Señor Diez. They leave home, no? Leave the family.

—Sometimes. It depends.

—Where you live in La Plata?

—53 Street, she says.

Some blocks away from the truth.

—Ah, a good street. Nearby the Institute. Maybe I come visit you, says Señor Diez.

Actually her flat is on not such a good street, on the fifteenth floor. It's high. She's never lived in a tower block before. There are two lifts to the flat, one to her front door and one to her back door, which face each other. The old lady who rents the flat out has left ornaments:

A china chicken on a doily
Glass animals
An iron swan
Pictures of Jesus
White plastic rabbit eating pink flowers
Bumpy plates attached to the walls
Nearly everything is cracked or has a lid missing. The old lady obviously knocks things over a lot. It reminds Moira of the woman in Boots, swinging her bag. One night she began drawing the bedroom curtains and there was the moon, pale in the middle of the window, and lying on its back as if it was something else the old lady had knocked over. More like a smile than a crescent. The most ordinary things can be strange; she had always thought a crescent was a sideways thing, a profile. But here even the moon is slanted differently. She thinks of time passing as it peels away, adds layers. She can count months this way.

—Dear Miss Douglas, Did you know that the moon is sideways-on here? I suppose the face is upside-down too, but I haven't looked yet. I wonder if you've had snow? It's getting hot here: people will have Christmas in shorts and eat oranges off the trees, rather than out of stockings.—
She never writes good postcards. She doesn't send the odd ones, in case people think she's cracking up.
—Here is Scotland – says Señor Diez, pointing at a map on the wall behind him.
—Yes – says Moira, and she feels close to the bitten outline, like looking at a friend's photograph.
—Maybe I come visit you in Edinburgh one of these days – says Señor Diez.
—One of these days: very good – says Moira
He offers her a lift in a brown Chevrolet. It has chips like bullet holes in the side panels.
—No thank you, I like walking.
He stares. There is a biro mark on his face. 'You will not be lonely? It is dark.'

—I'll be fine. Thanks.

—Maybe tomorrow I come visit your appartment.

—Yes.

The false address could be awkward. You end up with the same problems, no matter where you go. He walks towards her for a kiss and Moira clams up, makes herself cold. Like ice cubes. Is this how she has always looked? Señor Diez shuffles and puts another piece of chewing gum in his mouth.

—I like driving, he says, but I don't like flying. That's my problem.

He points at the sky.

Moira walks back watching the moon disappear and reappear round street corners. Almost as round as an orange now: nearly a fortnight since she saw it knocked over. The same moon, slanted differently.

Beautiful Fox

MOONLIGHT SHINES THROUGH the curtains but it doesn't wake the old man. He is awake already, having a conversation in his head. 'Hot this evening dear,' he is saying to his wife. 'Hot. I can't sleep.'

'Well, it's July,' says his wife. 'You should take that blanket off the bed.'

'Yes,' he says, 'I should do that', but he just lies there, in the square of moonlight, with his eyes open.

After a while he gets out of bed, pulls the drawstring tighter on his pyjamas and walks into the hall. It is so curious at this time of night. There are bookshelves on either side of him and they are like cliffs, blue and cold. The plants on the shelves hang their leaves out like the paws of nocturnal animals. His feet are bare and the floorboards are cold and waxy, but he can feel them better like that; he can avoid the ones that creak. He walks in a zig-zag to the kitchen, and his wife is still talking. 'Why don't you make yourself a cup of tea?' she is saying. 'It'll make you feel better.' He switches the kitchen light on and takes the kettle to the sink. On the wall there is a picture of a saucepan and some onions, re-appearing every ten tiles or so, like a recurring nightmare. He stares at the picture while the water runs.

There is a sound outside, a dog barking, or maybe it is even a fox; foxes come into the city these days but usually in cold weather, in the winter. They come and look for food. He and Jessica saw that fox once, one night in December, just gliding above the snow, and it was beautiful; they had stood, arm-in-arm, holding their breath, watching. Orange against white. That evening the snow had started falling, and the city had been covered up. He remembers the way the fox looked at them, the way it turned its sharp face.

The old man opens the cupboard and looks at tea boxes. There are so many of them. 'What shall I have?' he says. 'Shall I have Lemon Zinger? Do I want to be zinged at three forty-five in the morning? Or rosehip and apple? Or spearmint?' His daughter made some pasta thing with garlic last night, and garlic disagrees with him. It makes him feel bad in the middle of the night. He thinks the spearmint would be best for his stomach, but ordinary tea, that is better for his mind, for his heart. He lifts a mug off the mug tree and when the kettle has boiled he puts a tea-bag in the mug and stirs it around. He likes his tea nice and dark, not the kind his daughter makes; that is just white liquid. 'This is the land of milk and water,' says his wife, but no, it's not his wife, it's him saying that; his wife liked weak tea.

Everything sounds loud at this time in the morning, even sipping. Even the quietness is loud. The fridge clicks in its sleep, in one of its strange, freezing dreams, and it makes him jump. Tea falls on the lino. 'Hell,' he says, but there is no reply. His wife is not there any more; she has gone off again, suddenly, without telling him, she has just slipped away. 'Come back,' he says, but there is silence. Every time she disappears he is afraid she will not return. Cold air blows through his pyjama shirt, but the window is shut. The glass is black, black, reflecting nothing.

The old man walks with his tea into the sitting room. Living room, his son-in-law calls it, but his son-in-law does not live in it. 'Right,' the old man says to the hi-fi in the corner, to the rows of CDs, to the picture of boats in a harbour. 'What do I do now?' he says. He can hear a seagull screaming above the roofs. Night-time always has seagulls in it now but every time the screaming sounds new. He looks through the window and he can't see it for a while, the seagull, but then he does; it is standing, huge and truculent on the roof of the car mechanic's. '*Tired Of Your Tyres? Exhausted By Your Exhaust? Let Us Refresh*

You'. Does it say that in the adverts? Yes, he thinks it says that. 'Ah,' says the seagull, and it raises its grey wings and flies away. The sky is layered with clouds but it is going to be hot tomorrow, he can feel it.

When he turns round, he sees a woman standing in the doorway. She is wearing a red dressing gown, holding it around her as if she is cold.

'Dad?' says the woman.

'I just made myself a cup of tea,' says the old man.

'Are you all right, Dad?' says the woman. 'I heard you talking to someone,' she says.

She walks towards him. She has kind eyes; brown, brown, like chocolate. He loves his daughter, but sometimes he can't remember what her name is.

'You're crying,' she says.

'No,' he says. 'No, I'm not. Do you remember when we?'

'What?' she says.

'The fox,' he says. 'Do you remember when we saw the fox? That winter?'

'You should be in bed,' she says. 'You're tired.'

'No,' he says. 'It was beautiful.'

'I remember you and Mum telling me about it,' says the woman. 'I remember you sitting at the edge of the bed and telling me about it.'

'Yes,' he says, 'it was a beautiful fox.'

'Let's get you back to bed,' says his daughter, and she puts her hand on his arm.

There are things he wants to know. Why he is here, he wants to know that. Also where he is. He has worked out that he must be near the sea. This is a start. 'I'm just going outside for a minute,' he says. 'I just would like to be outside.'

'But you're only wearing pyjamas,' says the woman.

'So?' he says and he wonders how long ago it was that she grew up. He walks quickly into the hallway. The hallway smells of air freshener and garlic, a foreign smell. It makes him feel unwell. He turns the latch and opens the front door wide. He breathes. There is already light in the sky, a quiet, pink light, and

10

the seagulls are flying in swathes now, back to the coast. It looks as if they are pulling some big dark curtain with them as they go. The garden is losing whatever it has in the middle of the night; its sadness, and a square of yellow has appeared suddenly on the pathway. This means that the man, the son-in-law, is up; he is up and switching the light on and he will be downstairs any minute. He will be downstairs wearing Aftershave. 'Quick,' says the old man.

'What are you doing?' says the woman. She is standing behind him and holding onto his elbow, as if he is about to keel over. The old man does not reply. He peers into the green bushes at the end of the garden. Upstairs there is the sound of water running, and a radio. The radio is singing:

What Shall We Do With The Drunken Sailor
What Shall We Do With The Drunken Sailor
What Shall We Do With The Drunken Sailor
Ear-ly In The Morning?

'Yes', says the old man, 'there it is.'

He sees it suddenly; it is walking like treacle through the bushes. Soundless. A small, orange fox. 'See?' he says. 'See where I'm pointing?'

'Where?' says the woman. It is no use trying to stop him now. She remembers the way he used to point things out when she was small; how she would look the length of his blue-jumpered arm and into the sky, trying to see what he had seen. She had forgotten that: how much time she had spent with him, trying to locate things in the distance. 'Oh yes,' she would say, 'I can see it,' whatever it was, a butterfly or a bird of prey. And often she would pretend, just so she didn't look stupid.

'Can you see it now?' her father says, and he is still looking at something in the leaves.

'Where?' she says. She follows the stretch of his arm but her eyesight is not good in the dark and she can hardly even make out the gate, or the houses opposite. She will have to lie again, to make him happy; she will have to pretend that she has seen some animal moving quickly; some creature with glowing eyes.

11

'Look. There,' says her father, and she smiles. There is nothing. She stares hard into the flower-beds.

'Dad,' she says, and she sighs because she is trying to think of something else to say, something that won't annoy him or confuse him or make him sad, and it is so difficult seeing him like this, the way he is now; she is sighing because of that, when she hears her mother talking. Suddenly, for the first time in months, she can hear her mother, speaking in her slow way. 'Dear man,' she is saying, 'dear man,' and the words are so clear. She has missed her mother's voice more than anything.

'Can you see it?' her father is saying. 'Beautiful fox,' and his face has one tear, running diagonally. There is the noise upstairs of her husband shutting a door and beginning to walk downstairs, and before he gets to the hall and asks what they are doing, standing there letting all the air in, she says, 'Yes, yes I can,' because there is a fox, definitely, she can see it now, running away from them, away from the houses, something bright and good.

Left-Foot Loafers

T HERE WERE RUSSIAN sailors in town; all summer they had been roaming the streets in uniformed pairs. Their legs were bowed, just as people imagined sailors' legs to be, and they didn't take off their white hats. Everything about them was lonely and marine. They seemed to be searching for something, but they were always in the wrong end of town, the slow, supermarket end where nothing happened, where it was always the middle of the afternoon. They walked past the town's two chip shops, the Ocean Fry and the Deep Sea, and looked in at the battered, unrecognisable fish. Mary Singer's brother had taught her a Russian phrase once, and she always thought of it when she saw them. *Bozhomoy – Oh my God*. Maybe they were thinking that – *Bozhomoy* – when they looked at the town and its fish.

Mrs Knee, the cookery teacher, had been Miss Foot before she got married. She was lilac-haired and piggy-nosed, and her eyelashes were the colour of dry grass. Every Friday she explained some tedious domestic process, or drew an animal on the board and carved it into strange, cruel sections. Then she would start to shout, clapping her hands as rows of girls stared at her with drained faces.

'Pair up now please,' said Mrs Knee. 'Wash your hands and pair up.'

They had to work at the home booths. Home booths had a cooker, a cupboard and kitchen utensils. There was no sink;

13

you had to queue up for the sink. Mary shared her home booth with Linda Nugent at the end of the room. It was by the window. You could stare through the glass at the lavender and the playing fields and feel a strange, tugging need to be outside. Their school was called the Sacred Heart School for Girls and sometimes Mary wondered what a sacred heart was supposed to look like, whether it beat fast like hers, or was something muscly and unpleasant, like the organs that Mrs Knee drew on the board.

Since the beginning of term the cookery class had progressed from stuffed eggs to quiche lorraine. The recipe book gave the title curly lettering because it was in French, and there was a little drawing of onions at the bottom of the page, and a wee man with a moustache.

Linda Nugent tipped flour into a bowl, via a sieve, because Mrs Knee was watching them. Mary couldn't do it because she had purple ink on her hands and thick, black crescents of earth and sweat and desk-varnish beneath her fingernails.

'Did you tell your mum about missing maths?' Linda asked.

'No.'

'It's going to get worse, the longer you leave it.'

'No it's not.'

Linda seemed like someone much older than thirteen; bouncing and practical with big rubber-heeled shoes. 'You should take your friendship bracelet off, Mary,' she said. 'It's unhygienic.'

Linda was left-handed, and when they sat together, her head would lean towards Mary as she wrote. Occasionally her right hand flicked Mary's ear as she wound a curl of hair around her finger. While the quiches lorraines were cooking they had to write about refuse bins. Mrs Knee said that choosing the right bin was very important. She wrote this up on the board and they had to copy it down.

Choosing a Dustbin

Buy one made from plastic or strong galvinised iron if it is to be exposed to all weathers. Make sure that the lid is domed and fits tightly (to discourage flies and cats).

14

'Choosing a binette,' Linda recited, breathing like someone asleep.

Choosing a Binette
Remember that <u>plastic</u> *ones are preferable to* <u>metal</u> *because they do not* <u>rust</u> *and do not become* <u>chipped</u> *or* <u>dented</u>. *See that there is an effective* <u>pedal</u> *for raising the* <u>lid</u>.

You had to underline important words. Sometimes it was difficult to know where to stop; to know where the importance ended.

PRACTICAL WORK
Find <u>illustrations</u> *and* <u>prices</u> *of* <u>refuse bins</u> *made by* <u>three different firms</u>. *State* <u>which</u> *you would* <u>choose</u> *and* <u>why</u>.

Mrs Knee didn't call it homework, because 'practical' sounded more project-like and experimental. 'Practical' was exactly the right word for a home economics class.

'My mother doesn't do this,' said Mary. 'She doesn't sit at the kitchen table and write about refuse bins all day.'

'Mary,' said Linda, 'shut up.'

Linda could be very cruel sometimes; she could say things that made Mary's heart swing like a punchbag. Linda was so uncomplicated that Mary sometimes envied her. All you needed to do was tell people to shut up; that was all there was to it.

On Friday evenings Mary went to Linda's house and ate pancakes. The Nugents' kitchen had a yellow kind of cleanness to it: bleached tiles, checked tea-towels, slatted blinds at the window. The sun shone in in bright stripes.

'So,' said Linda as if she was still in the cookery class. 'We need flour, an egg, some oil and some milk.'

She had a way of talking that made Mary think of cartoon shows. Her words came out loud and slapping, as if she wanted to frighten something. Her front teeth stuck out, exaggerated, like a hamster's, and when she ate, she held her hands up in a little cupped shape.

On Fridays she strode around the kitchen proprietorially, opening cupboards.

'Does your mum mind you using the cooker when you're by yourself?' Mary asked.

'Of course not,' said Linda. 'Why, does yours?'

'No, I just wondered. Some parents mind.'

Linda made a strange clicking noise at the back of her throat, the kind of noise most people made when they were alone.

'What?' she said. 'What are you looking at me like that for?'

'I wasn't.'

Mary was only at Linda's for the pancakes. The clean, yellow house depressed her; if it wasn't for the pancakes, fat and undercooked, with caster sugar and lemon juice, she would never go there.

'When we've had tea we can watch telly,' said Linda. 'Or we could swim in the pool.'

Mary looked through the window at the pool, a bright blue rectangle in the middle of the grass. There were two sparrows playing in the puddles by the edge. If her parents had a pool, they wouldn't let her swim alone, but Linda was a bold child; maybe it was natural for bold children. Maybe that was why they built the pool in the first place. There was something curious about Linda anyway: the way she threw herself down hills and never hurt anything. She had pure white skin that never bruised or bled. Mary only had to lean her elbows too hard against a desk to leave a blue impression.

'I didn't bring my swimming costume,' she said.

'It's OK,' said Linda, 'I've got a spare one you can borrow.'

Mary tried to imagine herself there until six o'clock, seven o'clock, heavy with pancake and floundering in the Nugents' swimming pool, in Linda's spare costume.

'Let's just watch television,' she said.

'OK,' said Linda, but whatever Mary suggested, she always made it sound as if the other option would have been better. 'Why do you say *television*?' she said. 'It sounds stupid.'

She left the kitchen and came back after a couple of minutes

16

wearing her white sandals. They sat around her feet, anaemic-looking against her skin. They did not go with her school uniform.

'I always change into these when I come home,' she said, as if this was some fascinating piece of information.

They waited for the frying pan to heat up, then Linda cooked four pancakes expertly, quickly, tossing each one and putting them on two plates. 'You can start without me,' she said. 'I'm going to have chocolate sauce with mine.' She made sugar and lemon juice sound like a feeble choice of flavouring.

Linda's hair was blonde and wiry, like a dog's coat, and she always had a disinfectant smell about her. Maybe it was the soap in the Nugents' bathroom: bright yellow and cracked; about the only unhygienic thing in the house.

After they'd eaten the pancakes, Mary always went into the bathroom and waited: she could while away several minutes in there without having to talk to Linda. She stood behind the door and stared at the poster on it: a picture of a hedgehog in grass cuttings. The poster had always been there; it looked about twenty-five years old. On the shelf there was a plastic doll which smiled and hid a spare toilet roll under its big, voile skirt.

Mary began to count seconds. She heard the jingle of sandal buckles as Linda walked past the door and into the living room; the television was switched on, and there was the noise of laughter, but Linda was silent. She went into a strange state when she watched television; lifeless, like a dummy in a shop window. Mary calculated that she would have to spend twenty minutes in the living room with Linda. She unlocked the door.

'Aren't you going to tell your mum about Mrs Edwards?' Linda asked, with her back to Mary. She was staring, unblinking, at a green monster on the TV screen.

'Probably,' said Mary, 'but not today.'

Mrs Edwards was their maths teacher. She had reported Mary for skiving lessons. 'I wouldn't be at all surprised if you're not suspended,' she said. She was always talking in double negatives: two minuses made a plus.

Once, Mary said, 'Mrs Edwards, if I have minus eight cats,

say, and I have another minus eight cats, why do I suddenly have sixteen cats?' and Mrs Edwards had just stood behind her desk and made a strange kind of noise. For about three days, they had liked each other. Now, whenever Mary thought of her she felt as if someone had hit her hard in the stomach.

'Oh,' Linda said to the cartoon she was watching, 'Um,' and she grinned like a dog smiling and wound a lock of thick blonde hair around her finger.

'I don't care if I'm suspended. It would be great,' said Mary.

She couldn't understand why people like Linda got so worried about suspension, when it was such a chance for freedom. If she left school now she could do so many things: she could go and visit her brother in France; she could fly to Paris, then get a train to where he was staying. Fontainbleau: the name made Mary think of peacocks. At night, she worked out the journey in her head, but she kept getting stuck at the same scene, on a train outside Paris.

'I'd die if I got suspension,' said Linda, and she made it sound like an illness; like cholera.

Linda was always worried about homework: she always took it seriously, as if it mattered how neat the margins were. She changed out of her school uniform because her parents told her she had to, and she did this even when her parents were not there. She sat upstairs in her stuffy, sun-dancing bedroom, concentrating, for hours, with her slippers on.

Some uses that man has for water.
  It is used for watering the gardens with hoses.
  It is used in central heating systems.
  It is used in rivers for turning paddles inside mills, to grind up grain.

To illustrate her homework, Linda had cut out magazine-pictures of a woman in a shower and children in a swimming pool, and the teacher had written *8/10 – One Credit* at the bottom of the page. Mary chose the other homework option: *My Holidays Through the Water Cycle*, and wrote:

I am a small drop of water and I am in the air-bus (a cloud) going on my holidays through the Water Cycle. The cloud-driver says, 'Please put on your parachutes,' and we fall as precipitation to the ground.

At the end of her essay, the teacher wrote:

Illustrations? Imaginative, Mary, but not always correct. 6/10.

Mary's parents never seemed to buy magazines that she could cut pictures out of.

The cartoon was ending; a crowd of children with fixed hair stood in a circle and laughed. The green monster was eating hamburgers. When it chewed it made a repetitive gnashing sound.

'Well,' said Mary. She began to twirl the friendship bracelet that Linda had made for her. It was a braid of white, blue and yellow cotton. 'I suppose I'd better go now,' she said, and she tried hard to put reluctance into her voice.

'You always leave after ten minutes,' said Linda, not looking up from the television. 'You always leave. You just come here for the pancakes, don't you?'

'Of course I don't,' said Mary, and to prove it she sat down and looked at the magazines that were lying on the Nugents' glass coffee table. *The Field, The Sunday Times Supplement* and *Look-In*. She looked at the adverts in the back of *The Field*, because they always had intriguing pictures of women in hideous floral skirts and black and white illustrations of West Country cottages that families might want to spend their time in.

'Do you get *Look-In?*' Linda asked, and she began to sing the advertising jingle. 'La-la-la-la-la-Look-In,' she sang, 'La-la-la-la-la-Look-In. Hey Look-In, loo-ookin' good.'

'No,' said Mary, and she turned over another page. There was a 'woman-in-the-shower'-shaped hole in the paper. She recognised the outline.

After a while Linda got up and walked back out into the kitchen. Mary sat and listened to the sound of cupboards being opened again, cutlery chosen, lids taken off jars. There was a short pause, and then the clang of a spoon stirring something around a glass. Linda walked slowly back into the room with two glasses of banana milk-shake.

'I'm not meant to have this during the week,' she said, 'but what the hell? They won't be back till six.'

Mary had often heard Captain Nugent saying, 'What the hell.' He wasn't a real captain, just captain of the Salvation Army, but everyone in the town called him that. 'There's Captain Nugent,' they said, standing just a little way in from their windows as he walked past. Some people who didn't know the Nugents very well thought he really did work on a ship.

Linda drank her milk-shake in two gulping, gasping sessions. When she'd finished, she had milk on her waxy-white top lip. 'I love banana milk-shake,' she said.

Mary looked at the vast glass of cream froth. There was a transfer of a smiling mouse on the side of the glass. 'I'm really sorry,' she said, 'but I don't think I'm going to be able to get through it.'

'Why didn't you say before I made it?' said Linda.

'Because I didn't know you were making it.'

'I'll have to drink it then,' said Linda, and she picked up the glass and gulped once, twice, and put the glass down empty. 'I feel full now,' she said.

Mary looked at the clock on the mantelpiece. Three golden balls spun in a clockwise direction and then spun back again, silently.

'Mum and Dad are at Church Discussion Group,' said Linda, and she looked at her watch.

It was twenty past four, and sunny outside. Reflections from the swimming pool bounced, beautiful and white, against the ceiling. Sparrows were making their sad, suburban sounds in the Nugents' apple trees.

'I'd better go now,' Mary said, and she got up and walked towards the front door. Linda didn't follow her. She wanted to watch the end of something on another channel.

20

'Bye then,' Mary shouted from the hallway. 'Thanks for the pancakes.'

Linda did not reply.

It was a mile and a half back home, uphill. Linda's house was in a new estate that had shiny cars in nearly every driveway, and pale yellow roses growing from squares cut into the concrete. The front doors had fake bubbles in them, that reminded Mary of glass cow pats. All the houses were called Sea View and Sea Side and Seashore. The sea was four miles away. You couldn't see it from the estate.

She tried not to think of catastrophes as she walked, but she had a habit of counting her steps, and counting reminded her of catastrophe. *One, two, three, four, five, if I don't get to the lamp-post before eight, I will be run down by a lorry.* Linda told her she shouldn't believe in fate and that she should never read horoscopes. Things like that were twisted.

There was the sound of adults talking: a dull tide of male voices, and above it, higher, female attempts to be heard. Soon, the men and women would stop trying to talk to each other altogether, and separate into two groups at either end of the patio. These were the people her father talked about in the evenings. 'I am useful to them,' he said to her mother. 'That's why they don't want me to get promoted.'

'Of course,' her mother would say, agreeing vehemently, too vehemently for her nature.

Mary could hear her father speaking now, offering everyone a drink – 'Cynthia: Gin and tonic? Martin: A beer? Or a white wine?' and she could see her mother at the kitchen window, already pink in the face, pressing ice cubes into glasses. It was hot, but it was going to rain.

They were having a barbecue. She had forgotten that; she had said she would come home to help out with salads.

'Mary,' said her mother when she opened the door, 'every-one's here.'

She took a knife out of a drawer and gave it to Mary.

'How about making one of those tomato salads?' she said. 'Cut them into nice thin slices.'

'Can't I cut them into quarters?' said Mary, and her mother said, 'Yes, darling, cut them any way you want,' and she smiled because she didn't want to argue, not at that precise moment, because she could see Mrs Thompson and Mrs Wain standing outside the kitchen window in their lacy white dresses and their big flirty hats and their lipstick, smiling and waving at them as if they were animals in a zoo. Mary could tell that her mother wanted to rush out and steer them away from the smoking barbecue with its wobbling chrome leg. The wobbling barbecue was something of an obstacle when people came round to stand on the patio.

'Good day at school?' her mother asked.

She had her nervy smile on. She was wearing the black dress she had made, the Indian-looking one, and bangles that clinked every time she moved. She smelled of 'Opium'. This was not the moment to talk about skiving lessons.

'The Thompsons are here,' said her mother, 'and the Wains, and Mr Clive.'

Mary looked through the kitchen window and there they all were, standing on the patio, holding glasses. The sight of them made her stomach ache. She would have to go out and talk to them, and they would ask her about school. 'What subject do you like best? How long have you been there now? One year? Not long then. And whose class are you in? Lovely.'

Her mother sighed and put her hands on her hips.

'Please try not to run the taps unless you have to,' she said, then she smoothed her eyebrows into order, picked up a tray of drinks and went outside.

Mary got the sharpening steel out of the drawer and pulled the knife across it a few times, the way her father did before he carved chicken. She was not supposed to do this: her parents would hear the sound of the knife being sharpened up and imagine accidents, screaming, blood, but they would be fixed to the spot, a plate of chipolatas in one hand, a glass of wine in the other. Mary checked the blade carefully with her

22

thumb, and began to slice the tomatoes. *If someone comes indoors before I finish slicing this tomato, I will get suspension.*

She piled the cut tomatoes into a dish.

'Aren't you clever?' said Mrs Wain. Mary stared at her.

'Can you get my camera from the car, sweetheart?' her mother asked. 'It's so rare that we're all together,' she said, 'all in one place.'

'No it's not,' said Mary.

'No,' said her mother, looking at the fish pond as if she expected a whale to emerge, 'I suppose not.'

Mary found her mother's camera on the dashboard of the car. Even in the driveway there was a smell of burned sausages. From there she could look straight through all the windows of the house and see her parents sitting at the barbecue with Mr Clive, the Thompsons and the Wains. They were all balancing plates on their knees. As Mary walked towards them, she heard Mrs Thompson describing the Aztec blinds she had just hung in her bathroom.

'They're slatted,' she was saying. 'You know, the Aztecs would have had slatted blinds.'

'How interesting,' said her mother.

Smoke blew into their faces. Mary wished her brother was there. She felt lonely without him. She poured herself a glass of water, and imagined herself waking up the next morning. It was hard to imagine when this evening would be over; to really visualise how it would be.

'Isn't this nice?' her mother said.

Her father picked up the big green jug of Marguerita, and fished out a piece of lime.

'Lime,' he said. 'From the Arabic, *limah*.'

No-one responded. Mary gave the camera to Mr Wain. He had already drunk too much cider and his breath smelled of that and tomato ketchup and cigarettes. He talked too loudly with his mouth wide open.

'I click here do I?,' he bellowed, stepping back into the herb bed and standing on basil plants.

'Yes.' Her mother squinted in the smoke, her photo-face already arranged.

Mary sat on the wall. 'Could you mind the rosemary, Mr Wain?' she said. She had planted the rosemary herself.

Mr Wain didn't seem to hear. His big feet crushed a few more branches as he clicked the shutter. 'There,' he shouted. 'Ha ha ha.' Mr Wain was always laughing about nothing.

'Well,' he said, handing her mother the camera, 'one for the album.'

'Can I pass you some potato salad?' Mary's mother asked Mrs Thompson, who was staring into the fish pond; a huge, bleak heron, skewering chipolatas.

'Has it got spring onions in it?' said Mrs Thompson. 'I can't stand spring onions.'

'Well,' said her mother, 'it has, yes.' She put the bowl back down on the wall and smiled, and Mary suddenly wanted to cry; she wanted to put her arms around her mother and cry. Later, in the kitchen, she would try to joke about school, but it would not quite work.

'How have things got so bad?' her mother would say, frowning vaguely, drying a pyrex bowl, 'Why didn't you tell me before?' and it would be the worst criticism. Her parents were always concerned about her when she least expected it.

Monday came in square blocks.

French.

French.

Break.

Geography.

Lunch.

Maths.

Maths.

Break.

Maths.

Mary had coloured Break and Lunch a wonderful orange.

Halfway through geography, a large blonde girl came into the room with a piece of paper in her hands. She walked towards Mr Chapel's desk.

'Mary Singer,' said Mr Chapel, and he beckoned her with a crooked, signet-ringed finger.

'You have been summoned,' he said as she stood at his desk. Teachers who thought they were young and ironic and rather handsome always use words like 'summoned.'

'You have been summoned,' he said, 'to Mrs Gage's office.'

There was a subtle, almost imperceptible change to the room's noise level. Pencils were clutched to snapping point, the little pink erasers flicked and gouged by thumb-nails. Heads swivelled. Mary took the note from Mr Chapel. From his desk she could see things the class did not normally see. A wastepaper basket. An open drawer with an unfurling chocolate wrapper in it. Mr Chapel's trousers, up close, had a little tweedy fleck in them, like a jacket her father had.

'OK?' said Mr Chapel.

There was a noise in her head that sounded like a stampede, like a rushing wind, like the holy spirit that was always referred to in communion. *I will lift up mine eyes unto the hills from whence cometh my help.* She had never heard of anyone being summoned to the headmistress's office before. It was unbelievable; it was ridiculous.

'You have to go now,' said Mr Chapel. 'OK?'

And somehow she moved away from the tweedy flecks in his trousers, towards the door. She put her hand out, there it was, her hand, turning the handle, and Mr Chapel was already talking about rubber trees in Rio de Janeiro, about how people tied ropes around them and tapped them. She never thought she would want, one day, to hear about the tapping of Brazilian rubber trees. Her heart was turning into a galloping horse. From the corner of her eye she could see Linda Nugent staring at her, amazed, from their shared desk. Her face was blurred and as white as a candle. Beside her was Mary's exercise book, open at the page entitled 'The Riches of The Americas,' and there was Mary's geography text book with its innocent wee name, *Traveller's Tales,* and the picture of the happy boy and girl with rucksacks. What would happen to her papers and her text book? Who would care for them when she was gone? She felt as if she might be about to die. 'Good luck,' said Linda's mouth, but luck did not apply when you were visiting Mrs Gage. Luck did not come into it.

Mrs Gage's office was in the old building. The whole of Sacred Heart School was old, but Mrs Gage's office was in the oldest part of it, underneath the sweeping staircase. It was always dark under there, like the bridge in the Billy Goats Gruff. The door had a sign on it saying *Head*, and it always made Mary think of turnips for some reason. Maybe Mrs Gage's head reminded her of a turnip. Mary knocked on the door and hurt her knuckles.

'Come in,' said Mrs Gage's voice. She spoke immediately, leaving Mary no time to change her mind.

Mrs Gage was standing at the window like a fat gangster. She was wearing her beige crimplene, as usual, gathered in places by a meaningless brooch.

'Hallo, Mary,' she said, and she smiled, showing a set of regular teeth.

Mary's voice did not work. It felt as if she could only remain upright if she kept her mouth shut. If she spoke she would let go of necessary oxygen.

'Sit down,' said Mrs Gage, and she pointed to a very low chair which was positioned, gangster-like, so it faced the window. Mary sat down but the chair was lower than she expected. It was a trick chair, deluding her, letting her descend too far. She seemed to fall, out of control, for ten minutes, and when she eventually got to the seat, she was in precisely the right position for the sunlight to shine directly into her face.

'Now,' said Mrs Gage, 'Mrs Edwards has told me that you are not attending your maths classes.'

Mary's voice croaked from the depths of the chair. The sunlight was dazzling and white.

'I've only missed two.'

'Mrs Edwards told me it was five, and I do not believe that she is a liar. Are you telling me that Mrs Edwards is a liar?'

'No, but I only missed two.'

'So you are accusing Mrs Edwards of lying?'

'No.'

Mrs Gage seemed to be obsessed with the same idea. Mary couldn't see the point of her argument at all.

'Do you feel that Mrs Edwards is a fair teacher?' Mrs Gage asked, changing tack a little.

'No, I don't,' said Mary. 'What do you think?'

'I am asking the questions.'

Mrs Gage strutted around a little behind her desk. She had the kind of body that looked as if it was made from latex, like a fat bendy-toy. She sighed and picked up a window hook that was propped up in the corner of the room. She attached the hook to a catch in the sash window and lowered it. Air rushed in, along with the sound of seagulls and girls' screams.

'Is there any reason why you missed these lessons?' she asked, but she seemed preoccupied with lowering the window just the right amount.

'A friend of mine slipped on some cabbage in the dining hall and dislocated her elbow,' Mary said. 'I went with her to the medical room till her mother turned up.'

'But Mrs Clipper arrived at 1.10,' said Mrs Gage, finally casting aside the window hook and looking at a book on her desk. 'Maths does not finish until 1.40.'

Mary did not answer. She just sat on the low chair, with the sun in her eyes.

'Maths is important, Mary,' Mrs Gage said. 'You need maths to go on to A levels and to get into university.'

On the wall behind her head there was a sign saying:

'The words of the Lord are pure words: as silver tried in a furnace of earth.'

Below it there was a poster of a ginger kitten in a boot.

'Now,' said Mrs Gage, 'This is a serious matter.'

She walked towards her and for a moment Mary thought she was going to hit her. She bent so that she was nearly at chair-level, and handed her an envelope.

'This is for your parents,' she said. 'I need it back, signed, by the end of the week.'

She stood up to her full height again and one of her knee-bones cracked. She didn't say anything else, she didn't say 'That will be all' or 'You can go now,' but there was some communication between them, some telepathy sparking around the room which told Mary that she didn't want her in her office any more. She wanted her the hell out of there. Mary climbed out of the chair.

'Bye then,' she said. She couldn't think what else to say. Mrs Gage was already watering a trembling ivy with a little plastic watering can.

On her way home, she saw some Russian sailors loping around like ghosts in the distance, like her conscience. It had started to rain and they were sheltering in the doorway of a shoe-shop, beside a rack of left-foot loafers. The sailors watched her as she ripped Mrs Gage's letter up and threw it into a concrete bin.

On Tuesday there were curious rounds of grey lamb for dinner. Mary sat at one-eighth of an octagonal table with seven other girls, and they all stared like cattle at the reflections of their faces in the copper water jug. Mrs Knee and Mr Chapel and Mrs Gage and all the other teachers sat on the stage where the teachers always sat, so they could be looked up to.

'Could you pass the salt please, Mrs Knee?' Mary heard Mrs Gage say, from the depths of her beige cowl-neck.

'Certainly, Mrs Gage.' Mrs Knee's hair wobbled slightly, like a turkey's comb.

Somehow, everything the teachers said sounded like a conspiracy.

Mary used to eat sandwiches until she got mocked for the fillings. 'Your mum is one of those hippies that wear Jesus creepers,' she was told, as Carol Thwaite prised open her sandwiches one day without her permission, because she was two years older and it was her job to scare people. Mary had taken sandwiches with peanuts and apple puree in them, which tasted surprisingly good. But if you ate rounds of grey lamb, people thought you were normal, not bizarre and superior, sitting there with your strange sandwiches, in a different area of the dining hall.

The curly-haired school cook smelled of Fisherman's Friends and hated everyone. Mary had a kind of admiration for her. 'Christ!' she shouted, making Mrs Gage wince, and flinging semi-mashed swede onto people's plates. The swede slid into the gravy and formed a cloudy sludge, and some of the girls at Mary's table started to sing:

Most highly flavoured gravy, Glo – o – oo – ri – a.

'That is quite enough, girls,' Mrs Gage shouted in a voice that virtually split Mary into two halves.

When the teachers had left the dining hall, Mary scraped her dinner into the canteen bucket marked *Leftovers* and walked into town. She spent afternoon registration wandering nervously around the streets, praying that she didn't meet any teachers. She walked quickly into the centre of town, past the ranks of dahlias in people's front gardens, the cut-off conversations, the smell of mince frying, the shoe-repairers windows that said WE S-T-R-E-T-C-H SHOES, and she felt that maybe everything would merge together one day, form a big mass and mean something. Signs jutted out from billboards and windows all the way into the High Street, as if they were trying to tell her something, but they weren't; they didn't.

It took twenty minutes to walk from the Sacred Heart to the shopping centre. *If I can get across this road in four steps it will be OK.* She always gave her superstitions enough leeway for things to turn out all right. Soon she grew bolder and, at about the time people were leaving school for the day, she bought herself a cup of sweet, frothy coffee and some blue mascara called *Gentle Navy*.

Mary's father came home late, after she and her mother had already eaten supper. Mary was in her room when she heard him walk through the front door. She listened to the sound of their conversation, and somehow she knew they were talking about her. It was the quiet pitch of their sentences, the edge of surprise. After a while she heard them walking around the rooms downstairs, opening doors and there was the sound of their footsteps going into the living room. She could tell they were standing by the window, just standing there, with their eyes glazed.

Mary reached her arms out of bed and switched the radio on. A Norwegian woman was telling a strange story, about how she had lost her wedding ring in a forest twenty years ago, and how, one day, her husband had gone into the forest to shoot an elk and they found the ring inside the elk. It had been inside the elk for fifteen years. It sounded like a typical fairy story: there was always a hunter who went into a forest and shot something that was perfectly happy.

The phone rang late, about ten o'clock. She thought it might be her brother phoning from France, but it was Linda Nugent.

'So,' said Linda. 'What happened? You could have phoned. Did you get suspension?'

'No.'

'Did you see Mrs Gage again?'

'No.'

'Oh.'

There was a noise in the background of something hissing; Mary wondered if it was the Nugents frying pancakes. Linda sighed and made the strange clicking noise at the back of her throat.

'Did you remember to buy some material for needlework tomorrow?' she asked.

'Sorry, I forgot.'

'I knew you would.'

'Sorry.'

'You're useless,' Linda said and she hung up.

Linda was late arriving at the bus stop the next morning, because she had had to stop at Material World to buy a length of fabric. Captain Nugent drove her up in a large white Volvo, seconds before the bus arrived. There was a crucifix hanging from the driving mirror. Before she walked up the bus's steep little staircase, Mary caught a glimpse of Captain Nugent's blue jacket and brass buttons. He was also wearing a little badge saying *Jesus Loves You*. As soon as Linda got out of the car he drove off, fast, disappearing down one of the town's wide, plain streets. He didn't wave, the way her parents did.

Mary wondered if he was going to another prayer meeting.

Captain Nugent was the only one in naval uniform now; the genuine sailors, the real, Russian ones had left town at the weekend; they were sailing away on some big, lonely boat, laughing about the town they had just visited. It was strange how she missed them.

Mary chose a seat that she thought Linda wouldn't notice, that she might blunder past, but she found her instantly. The grey-carpeted cushion was unbalanced and rose slightly, like a see-saw, when Linda sat down.

'So didn't your parents get a letter or anything?' Linda asked, as if their phone conversation the previous night had never finished.

'No.' Mary found lying curiously easy. She had a talent for it.

'God,' said Linda. 'Don't you care about going to see Mrs Gage?'

'No.'

'My parents would kill me.'

'Would they?'

'You don't talk much these days, do you?'

Linda sat back, readjusting Mary's position as she did so.

'You ought to wash that friendship bracelet,' she said. 'Look, it's all grimy. It's really disgusting. I wouldn't have given it to you if I thought you were going to let it get all grimy.'

Mary didn't reply. She looked through the window at the route she had looked at for the whole of her life. They were at the crossroads by Pete's Garage now. It was raining a warm, summer rain. The same man in overalls was wheeling tyres around. She started to count them.

'Did you know that the spots on your face make a diamond shape?' Linda said. 'Or a cross.'

Mary swore at her and thought of Jerusalem donkeys, marked for life with the sign of the crucifix. The year before, the Sacred Heart school had put on an opera called *A Green Hill*. Mr Chapel had sung the part of Jesus, and all the girls had been photographed in their school uniforms for the programme, all except Mary, who had been at the dentist. 'You'll regret it one

31

day,' said Mr Chapel, stroking his Jesus-type beard, but she knew she wouldn't, just as she didn't regret Mrs Gage's letter, lying in four pieces in a bin by the discount shoe store.

The bus drove them inexorably towards the Sacred Heart. It was Wednesday morning. Linda sighed. 'I might as well talk to the wall,' she said, and after a while she turned around and knelt on her seat to talk to the girls behind them. She showed them the fabric she had bought in Material World. 'It's poplin,' she said. 'Feel it.'

'Lovely,' said the girls. 'What are you going to make?'

When Linda sat down again, Mary said, 'Do you know what the Russian is for 'Oh My God?' She paused. '*Bozhomoy*,' she said. She tried to sound as Russian as possible. Linda frowned. 'You say some really stupid things,' she said, and Mary knew that something inevitable was happening; that something, finally, was falling away.

Gloves

JACK GASPS AS he tramples into my car, his feet hovering above the bills and receipts. Drifts of paper are piled up on the rubber foot-mat.

'I must clear it out,' I say. 'I must clean it.'

I am shaking as I look for my keys; out of the corner of my eye I can see him looking in the wing mirror, like a co-pilot. My hand is a few inches away from his leg.

People have called this car a mobile skip. They have commented on the moss that grows along the window ledges, the bags of wine bottles that clank on the back seat, waiting to be recycled. There is seagull crap on the windscreen, an unromantic brown and white streak a few feet away from Jack's face. 'Quite an ecosystem,' he says. Neither of us comments on the seagull crap.

'Did you enjoy the film then?' he says. When he turns to look at me, his left ear lobe has a little fronze of moonlight around it. I want to move my arm and touch his face but we still don't know each other very well; we have just spent the last two hours sitting in the dark, making sure that our knees didn't brush. I bought a sherbet dip because I wanted something to calm my nerves but I ended up choking on the sugary dust. Jack slapped me on the back for quite a while, and I had tears running down my face. When I look in the driving mirror, I can see grey smudges under my eyes.

'It took me a while to get into it,' says Jack. 'The first half was quite slow, I thought.'

'Yes.'

I nod. I can't think what else to say. It was one of those films where everyone talked too fast, and the camera kept diving around, hunting for expressions. People ran about in green medical uniforms and said things like, 'What in hell's name is *that*—?' or 'We only have six minutes until it explodes.'

'Well,' I say. I can't remember much about it now, even though it finished less than quarter of an hour ago.

'Not very good really, was it?' says Jack, and I want to kiss him just to see what it feels like, the edge of his ear where the tiny hairs stand out.

We are parked here in a little alley just at the back of the cinema. No-one knows about this place but it's easy to find; you just turn off the main road and drive under the archway, the wheels jarring over cobbles, and once you're here you can stay all day. You can do your shopping, meet friends, see a film, go to Glasgow and back, and you won't have a little checked sticker on your windscreen when you return. Although a friend of mine parked in a place like this once, and found that they had put meters up while she was away and stuck a ticket under the wipers. When I tell Jack this, he laughs.

'Traffic wardens,' he says. He relaxes a little. He stretches his legs out and scrumples up the bits of paper.

Before Jack, I was with a man, the only man I've ever known who knew nothing about cars. 'What car is this?' he would say to people as he got into the passenger seat. The steering wheel would have the car's emblem on it; there might even be the name of the car somewhere in the front, but he just didn't notice. I was with him for seven years but it seems less now. Sometimes I find myself talking about him in the past tense as if he is dead. His name was David.

This is the first time a man has been in the car since David. He is taller and his knees go further. I can't believe how long

34

Jack's legs are: they make mine look like a child's when I sit next to him. He wears smart clothes, laundered things without cat hair, things that he probably places on coat hangers and puts away properly in a wardrobe. He works in an architect's office, but I haven't seen any of his drawings. Tonight I am taking him back to his flat, and he has said he will show me his work. He is working on an elevation. I almost say something about me coming up to see his elevation, but I bite my lip just in time. Instead I say, 'That will be nice.'

'What?' says Jack. He looks puzzled.

'That will be nice,' I say quickly, and I put the key in the ignition.

It is very cold now. Even though we are sitting inside the car, we can see the breath in front of our mouths. Dragon breath. Jack rubs his palms together, a dry papery sound.

'Apparently it's going to snow tonight,' he says.

'Is it?' I say. 'That's good. I like snow.'

'Ahhh,' says Jack. 'Sweet.'

I wonder how old he thinks I am. I wonder if he is as bad as me at judging age. I wind the window down a little because we are steaming up. The windscreen has a white coating on it that it is difficult to see through. I turn the key in the ignition and nothing happens.

'Oh,' I say.

I turn the headlight switch but there is no light. The car is as dark and unresponsive as a telephone box. The brightest things in it are Jack's eyes, glistening. I want to swear but I don't. I say, 'That's odd.'

'Left the lights on, did we?' says Jack. The moon has gone behind a cloud and his ears no longer have their halo.

'I am sure I didn't leave the lights on,' I say. 'I never leave the lights on. I always make sure I don't leave the lights on,' I say. Suddenly, I feel like crying.

'Does the radio work?' says Jack. He bends forward and twiddles the radio dials. Everything is black and silent.

'Great,' I say.

There are two pieces of wire hanging near the steering wheel, by my knee. When I join the ends together, there is a feeble flicker from the car light above our heads.

'There must be a short circuit,' I say.

'I don't think so,' says Jack. 'I don't think that has anything to do with it.'

We get out of the car. There is ice on the cobbles and our shoes make a crunching sound. We lift up the bonnet lid and look inside. It always alarms me to see a car exposed like this: to think that I am driving around inside something that looks like a vacuum cleaner.

'Hmm,' says Jack, and he pokes at a few pieces of coil and plastic. He says, 'I think it's the battery,' and something starts to ache behind my ribcage. I wanted to be sexy, sitting flippantly behind the steering wheel, driving with the colour of sodium streetlights waving across our faces. I wanted to put on my glasses and drive. Instead we are standing here in the cold, outside a closed cinema. A man with a limp walks through the staff exit and bolts it shut for the night. He stares at us for a second then limps off, underneath the archway. By now, we could have been sailing along the dark streets towards Jack's flat. I could have put the radio on or perhaps my new Lou Reed tape, the one I bought that has nothing to remind me of anyone. Instead, we are standing here. This part of town is exposed at night, full of fences with hexagonal holes in them and concrete structures that would make instant snowmen. It is nearly midnight, and there is only the sound of a taxi, lonely as the whistle of an aeroplane.

Jack says, 'Let's just leave the car here.' He says, 'No-one would bother to nick it if they had to jump start it first.'

'Damn,' I say. I am not listening to him.

I lock all the doors, wishing I was in there, driving home, without him. And we walk. Back to his flat, in the dark, not touching. I am wearing a new pair of gloves. Inside there is a label that says the queen buys the same make. They make me feel expensive, as if I am exotic and perfumed, with a good haircut.

'Nice gloves,' says Jack.

We walk through the park, taking the narrow paths that follow slopes religiously. We ascend and descend small hills for no reason, breathing warm air out, our feet scraping against the gravel. Jack talks about the film. He talks about the film over a distance of five beech trees and three lamp-posts. 'U-huh,' I say, every once in a while. 'U-huh.'

Finally Jack says, 'I don't know – I didn't really get into it.'

'Never mind,' I say, and we walk silently on. I step loudly to make up for my lack of speech. I feel as if I have swallowed something, some thick medicine that prevents me from speaking. Jack says Hmm occasionally to fill in the silence. I can see his sighs in the air. He says he will walk me home, as I haven't got the car now. He says I can go to his flat another evening.

We descend the last small hill and walk towards the middle of the park. Jack strides slowly but it gets him an awful long way; I have to trot to keep up. I think we must look like something out of Billy Smart's Circus. In the distance there is a man roaming about carrying a bottle; the only figure on the horizon, the only other person in the park. Jack clears his throat and I can see him clenching and unclenching his fists. My heart feels tight just looking at this man. I am holding my keys and I turn them so that all the metal points outwards, like a dagger. I have read articles on self-defence and I always do that now; sometimes I notice I am doing it in broad daylight when I am walking past law-abiding citizens. This man couldn't defend himself anyway. He is old and short. He has greasy grey hair and bloodshot eyes. When we reach him he hovers in front of us and stares like someone about to fall over. We stop walking, and wait for him to speak.

'There's acid behind the gravestones,' he says.

'Aye, right,' says Jack, and we dodge around him, wrong-foot him. In front of us, just behind the trees, is the university library, illuminated like a temple by fluorescent light. I can see empty rooms full of bookshelves.

'That your girl?' says the man. 'That your woman?'

'Goodbye,' says Jack. I wish he had answered the man's question, then I might have known what to do; what to make of this whole evening. We move on as if we are on castors. I can hear the man mumbling behind us, kicking something.

'It's going to snow,' he shouts. 'It's going to snow.'

My first boyfriend was called Luke, but his name doesn't matter now. He was a tall, bony sixteen-year-old.

One day we took a bus into town and sat in a tea-shop that was called Choice. The name was written backwards in fat writing on all the windows. ECIOHC. It was also reflected in mirrors. If Luke had been older maybe he would have said something about being spoilt for choice. But he was not. He gulped and his Adam's apple put me off my tea. Choice had doilies underneath everything but it was also modern and self-service, and it seemed quite sophisticated. It had things like baked potatoes and soup and croissants. We ate croissants copiously and groped for things to say, staring at each other on opposite sides of a small, round table.

Luke was allergic to my perfume and he sneezed all day. When we kissed on the floor of my bedroom he had to turn his head once in a while to sneeze, his bony chest digging into mine. I was wearing a black T-shirt and a tight skirt that I had dyed an uneven red. My best friend said I looked like a tart but I didn't believe her. Luke whispered that I looked like a gypsy woman, which was more the effect I wanted. I had just had my hair permed and I think I looked most of all like Kevin Keegan, but Luke told me I looked like a gypsy and I believed him for a while.

'The flat's an awful mess,' I tell Jack when we get to the pedestrian crossing. I can see it from here. My flat-mates have left the living room light on.

'You should see my place,' says Jack, but I don't believe he lives in the state that we do. I will have to invite him in for a coffee and he will see the worst of it: the ashtrays spilling out over the cracked formica, the plastic bags taking up space for no reason in the open cupboards, the iron-shaped mark on the carpet. 'I'm looking for a new place actually,' I will say, trying to find two clean mugs from the cupboard above the sink.

The snow starts falling just before we reach the front door. It is so silent it could break your heart. The flakes seem magnetised to Jack's coat and they just sit there on the dark wool. It takes ages for them to melt.

'So,' I say, hanging onto the door-knob as if it is an elevator button and will transport me somewhere, suddenly: as if I will just vanish. My heart is bashing against my ribs now – I am surprised he can't hear it. So. Jack stares at the foot-scraper. He has rather a large nose actually but nice dark hair. The snow falls into it like snow in a film, and I want to say something kind but I can't bring myself to. Now we are here, coffee is out of the question. I can imagine my flatmates sitting up there in the kitchen like condors, watching late night TV on the portable. There will be a smell of rubbish bins and rancid butter. There will be empty cardboard boxes and pieces of bread with bites taken out of them. There will be card decks and tea rings.

'Are you doing anything next Friday?' says Jack and I say, 'No. Nothing planned.' So non-committal. We clench our teeth and speak roughly, as if we hate each other.

'Right,' says Jack. 'I'll phone you then.'

'OK.' We don't kiss: we just shuffle.

'Right,' says Jack again. 'Hope you get the car fixed,' and I watch him turning and walking away, past the kebab shop, with his cold hands in his pockets. It will take him ages to get back to his flat; it is right on the other side of town. I can already see his endearing traits; the way he walks slightly pigeon-toed, slightly off-centre. But I don't think my heart will ever be full. Not to breaking point.

Mr Hessel Buys Wine Gums

THE MANAGER DOESN'T show up much. If he does, it is always when we are busiest. He hangs around the tills, breathing. He says little but his fat fingers drum against the counter, as if he is counting customers. When he speaks the words seem to come through his nose. 'Fine,' he says. 'Great.' He has a bald head with a few black hairs clinging sadly to it. He sighs. Then he wanders away again, to wherever he goes in the afternoon.

The supermarket is called Showy but it's small and dismal. Around one o'clock people turn up for things to put in sandwiches. This is the only shop on the street so we get people who would normally go to a deli for pastrami on rye. Here they get Spam on Mother's Pride. Some workmen arrive to buy pork pies. There are five of them and they are all short and wear hard hats. Four of them call me 'darling' and the last one calls me 'pal' because that's what he always says to his mates and he forgets to change the word.

'That's OK,' I say and I raise my eyebrows at Rita when they have gone.

'Couple short of a six-pack,' says Rita across the tills then she lights up a cigarette. When we start talking she always rummages underneath her overall and finds a packet of Dunhills. We are not meant to smoke here but she doesn't care.

'Quick cig,' she says.

A customer puts a packet of mints at one end of the conveyor belt and we watch silently while it sails like driftwood up to the other end. This is a bad supermarket, but it is good for sweets. We have jelly babies and liquorice sticks and sugared almonds. We have dolly mixtures, gob-stoppers, mints and wine gums. An old man called Mr Hessel comes in every day to buy wine gums. He never buys anything else. I found a split packet last week and they were chewy, like eating flavoured slugs.

Rita leans back on her chair, inhaling smoke. She takes long drags like a rebel, and stares through the window. 'So,' she says after a while. 'How's your cat?'

Rita likes talking. She likes to know how my cat is getting on, so I tell her anecdotes.

'Yesterday,' I say, 'I put some apricots in a bowl and she dragged them out again with her claws. She just started pushing them round the floor.'

I hadn't stopped her because she was having fun. The apricots had just rolled soft and helpless around the carpet and she had pounced on them with her legs out straight; I suppose the apricots had a kind of blood in them.

'They'll mess up your carpet,' Rita says. 'Fruit juice is impossible to get out.'

'I know,' I say, 'but she was enjoying herself.'

'How long have you had this cat?' she says.

'Not long,' I say. 'Six months.'

'Tabby, isn't it?'

'Yeah.'

'We had a tabby once when I was a girl,' says Rita. 'We called him Crisp.'

'Why?' I say.

'God knows,' says Rita, and she flicks her cigarette and goes to put some music on. That's the one good thing about working here – you can listen to music over the loudspeakers. We are meant to put on 'soft music' but the boss comes in so rarely that we bring in our own records. Working at the till seems more intriguing if you are listening to 'Echo Beach.' You feel sexy and mysterious, even when you are pricing tinned grapefruit. Rita chooses a record, turns the volume up then slinks back down the soup aisle.

41

'I think I might get myself a kitten,' she says. 'A little ginger one.'

'Ginger kittens,' I say, 'are sweet.'

The weather is bad all morning and by the afternoon it's black outside. It's black and raining. We must look like a fairy tale – the only illuminated thing for miles. People slosh past the window and stare at our signs. Spaghetti Hoops 26p a tin, Mandarins in Juice 45p a tin. The signs have Showy's logo, thin red lines, around the edges.

'This weather,' says Rita, 'is giving me a cold.'

She pulls a handkerchief from her sleeve and blows her nose. I think I'm catching something too – I can feel it, a kind of unhealthiness behind my skin, the start of a sore throat.

When the lunchtime crowd has gone I say, 'I'm going to make tea,' and I go to the back of the shop where the kettle is. The sink is under the window and I stare outside while the kettle fills. Showy must be the only supermarket that has a back garden, and Rita and I used to take it in turns to sit out there during the summer: it was peaceful and you could hear birds singing. Rita would leave smoke and cake crumbs in the grass. Now the garden is soaking wet – rain bends the leaves down, pours out of the overflow, creates mud. A blackbird leaps through the grass and pulls up worms.

I find a spare cigarette lighter on the window-sill and it works OK. The lighter is advertising something called Toby's Ale. 'Drink Toby's Ale,' it says, 'Always A Fine Choice.' There are so many things I don't know. I light the gas, put the kettle on and then the room goes dark. It just goes black suddenly as if someone has switched the light off. And the music stops, losing speed and getting lower, changing from a woman's voice to King Kong's, the way it does when you kick the plug out of the stereo.

Echo Beach, far a-way i-n t i m e

'Power cut,' shouts Rita from the shop. Her voice sounds loud in the dark. 'Bloody marvellous,' she says.

For a moment I wonder why the kettle is still working then

I realise it's on a gas ring. I stand and watch the blue circle it makes, like something exotic in the dark. It makes me feel good, somehow, that we can still have tea. We don't have to abandon hope. Rita appears at the doorway looking excited but trying to sound annoyed. 'Great,' she says. 'Bloody marvellous.'

'There wasn't even a thunderstorm,' I say, and we stare, both trying to make out each other's eyes. Rita is illuminated by the light coming through the window. She is silver round the edges, and I can see her 'R' necklace shining.

'Isn't it quiet?' says Rita. 'That music was pretty loud.'

I find a packet of candles and light a few. Then I walk up each aisle, dripping a bit of wax onto the shelves and fixing the candles down. They are rose-scented and everything is in this holy kind of glow. It's like a church service. There are soft circles of light, illuminating things as if they are significant. Packets of supernoodles, banana surprise baby food and economy washing powder. We stand for a while at the window drinking tea and watching people without umbrellas. Rain is like an enemy, when you look at their faces. It makes them frown. They could be really happy but the rain just makes them frown.

'Pissing down,' says Rita.

I don't answer but I think of the ways you can describe rain. It can piss, bucket, tip, pour, sheet, fall. There are not half as many descriptions for the sun. The sun shines.

'I suppose,' says Rita, with her eyes wide and vacant, 'I suppose we'll have to go home then. Sad eh?'

She sucks at her cigarette and the orange tip gets brighter. The smell of Dunhill mixes with the rose candles.

'No point hanging around,' says Rita. 'We can't even cash up.'

Then someone opens the shop door and she raises her eyebrows; I can see them moving.

'Someone's a bit keen,' she says, and we look to see who it is. It is the boss. He never normally comes in but he chooses today, when we have just illuminated the place with scented candles, as if we're in the middle of a seance. He looks strange in the dark – a small shape in a black suit. His white hands shine. 'What's going on?' he says.

I would have thought it was obvious. 'We're having a power cut,' I say. 'That's why we got the candles out.'

'But the wax will drip over everything,' he shrieks, running to the pasta section and prising a candle off the shelf.

'People couldn't see anything,' I say.

The boss twists the candle round in his hands. It is the same thickness as his fingers. He looks unhappy and the candlelight bounces against his baldness. It makes me wonder if he has ever gone for a romantic dinner with anyone and I feel sorry for him. He is just about to say something when the door opens again and Mr Hessel walks in. He looks around at the blackness, mumbles and shuffles up to the sweety racks. We hear rustling. There is the sound of a bag being dropped then after a minute or so he walks towards us with a packet of Seaworld Animal Shapes.

'Afternoon, Mr Hessel,' Rita shouts. She shouts because she thinks he is deaf. 'Nice afternoon.'

'A bit dark,' says Mr Hessel. He is wearing black trousers with green side seams – that's what they look like anyway, in this light. He makes a strange gasping noise with his throat.

'Seaworld Animal Shapes,' says Rita, peering at the packet. 'Is that what you want? You don't want wine gums?'

'Aye, I want wine gums,' says Mr Hessel. 'Are those not wine gums?'

'No,' says Rita, 'these are Seaworld Animal Shapes.'

'Oh,' says Mr Hessel.

I take a candle up to the sweet section and locate a packet of wine gums.

'Quite romantic in here, isn't it?' Rita says to the boss. Their faces light up with shadows, like masks.

'Are you having a power cut or something?' says Mr Hessel. The boss's nose whistles.

'Nah, we just thought we'd have a change,' says Rita. 'It makes shopping more interesting don't you think?'

The tills don't work but Mr Hessel always has the right amount for his wine gums: 42p. He pays and opens the door. He looks into the sky and it is lighter now. Grey instead of black. The rain sounds like the sea under car wheels.

'People will think this is a restaurant with all those candles,' he says. 'They'll be coming in for smoked salmon.'

'We've got pilchards,' I say. Mr Hessel closes the door.

'Well,' says the boss, 'I'm sure they'll switch the power back on in a minute.' And we lean against the still conveyor belts and wait. If he had arrived five minutes later we wouldn't have been here. The boss says nothing, just moves his fingers backwards and forwards, counting something. The smell of roses makes me sleepy.

'Quite romantic really,' Rita says again.

After about ten minutes, the strip lights flicker back and start to hum. The supermarket is suddenly very bright and makes us blink. Over the loudspeakers the music revs back up to speed. I'd forgotten about the music. A woman is singing 'My job is very boring I'm an office clerk . . .' It is extremely loud. 'We'll turn that off if you don't mind,' says the boss, and he strides on his short legs to the back of the supermarket.

When I go in the next morning, Rita is sawing wax off the shelves with a blunt knife.

'No bloody sense of humour that man,' she says.

She gets out her Dunhills. 'Quick cig,' she says.

She offers me one, which she has never done before. 'It was good fun yesterday,' she says.

Around midday, Mr Hessel comes in for his wine gums. 'Back to normal then,' he says.

'Afraid so,' says Rita.

The workmen come in at lunch for more pork pies. There are six of them this time and today one of them calls me hen and the others call me darling. When they've gone Rita whispers to me across the tills, 'In case you're wondering, the boss took the stereo. He just took it away last night after you'd gone..'

I stare out of the window and don't reply. There is nothing more to say; there is not even music now, to make me feel mysterious. I can hear Rita talking and I haven't got the energy to reply. I've run out of anecdotes.

'Your cat still chasing fruit?' she is saying, and I think of the squashed apricots I found all over the carpet when I got back home last night. Ingrained. Almost impossible to get out.

These Blocks Are Actually People

TEACHERS. ON EXCURSIONS we sit at the front of the bus and look so vulnerable, don't we? – like armadilloes without shells. The girls behind us are very quiet and regard the backs of our heads, looking for white hairs. I can sense it.

'Toffee?' says Mr Pretty as soon as we have cleared the school playground. He rustles a paper bag at me but I shake my head and tell him it is too soon after breakfast. Actually I didn't have any breakfast, I overslept. Mr Pretty scuffles the bag back in his lap and looks out of the window. He possesses very large eyebrows and a head full of sayings, one of which is 'long time no see,' another of which is 'do what I say, not what I do.' He says these to his pupils. I have heard people whisper that he is having an affair but this is hard to believe; schools are full of rumours and moral outrage, shocking, shocking in minds so young. Mrs Gerard sits across the aisle and ignores us. She does not like me because I do not have an artistic soul. I dissect frogs and wear T-shirts from Poundstretchers.

Mr Pretty leans across me saying, 'Toffee?' and she accepts one. They both roll the sweets round their mouths like chipmunks.

It rains mildly. The bus drones and smells slightly plastic, and at the moment it is quiet – early morning makes everyone pale and unresponsive. We just sit in a stupor with unfocused eyes, like duplicates of Count Dracula at dawn. Only the girls behind

47

us are talking, comparing sandwiches. 'Tuna mayonnaise, I've got tuna mayonnaise in mine,' one of them says. 'What have you got?'

'I've got . . .' and there is a sandwich-prising pause. 'I've got sandwich spread.'

'Oh.'

Most pupils have sandwiches in violent-coloured tupperware; some have packets of biscuits and those with street cred have nothing at all; the plan is to eat cheesy croissants in the gallery restaurant.

After a few minutes Mrs Gerard says, 'Who's going to do the head count?'

Oh dear, Mr Pretty and I appear to be suffering a temporary hearing loss. Mrs Gerard sighs and clumps to her heels. 'I suppose I'd better do it then,' she says, swaying inflexibly down the aisle, pointing her fingers at people and counting in twos. When she returns she gets out her notebook and writes the number with a fountain pen.

We are about halfway there when the bus driver switches off Radio One and finds a tape of Eric Clapton. There are shrieks of horror from every seat, but the driver is stubborn. He hates school trips. He hates youth. He looks like a tree-trunk, ingrained with hate lines, and Eric Clapton stays on, saying we look wonderful tonight. I notice that Mrs Gerard is a bit dreamy now. She gazes at buildings and her toe taps the song's rhythm. She has peculiar standards. She orders vests direct from Paris because they keep their shape much better. She told me that once in the staffroom.

I make classic mistakes. I am always calling pupils the wrong names because they remind me of people I used to know. Some teachers manage it, but I never feel quite convinced in this role; it never matters enough to me. School is just a woolly cave of people shouting. You have to act professional, sarcastic, versed in First Aid and fights, and I have this ironic image in which I am a large woman with a practical handbag, but sometimes the image scuttles away somewhere and leaves me, exposed, mouthing like a catfish in the playground. I shriek in a voice that isn't mine. In class I say, 'Have you been listening, Garry? Then perhaps you could explain the term transpiration for us,' and my voice waves across the room like the beams from a lighthouse.

As soon as we reach the gallery it starts raining hard. Mrs Gerard asks the driver to take us all the way up to the door but he says, 'Nowhere to turn round,' and he sits on his little round seat, staring at the windscreen wipers. Eric Clapton is singing 'Cocaine.' Everyone gets up from their seats, thuds down the steps and runs, heads covered with tupperware and books. Mrs Gerard says, 'Umbrellas are obviously de trop this year,' and Mr Pretty and I giggle obediently. She snaps out a large black umbrella with a wooden handle and we totter like the three stooges, crammed inelegantly under the spokes. We are already miles behind the pupils, who wait near a sculpture of 'Reclining Woman,' dry and laughing.

Inside, a warden dressed in black with lined grey shoes creeps very slowly towards us and gives instructions. No touching paintings. No running. No noise. No umbrellas. No photographs. No eating. No drinking.

He says, 'Any questions?'

And Michael Douglas says, 'When is the café open?' Michael Douglas from the fifth form. Not the famous actor. But he is witty and blond. Girls giggle and stand accidentally too near him. There are of course comparisons with the filmstar.

'Well, Michael,' says Mrs Gerard, putting on the ironic teacher face. 'We are here ACTUALLY to look at paintings not to spend the morning in the café.' And she swirls off into Room 1. She is wearing abstract earrings, as if she's cut out little pieces from a Miro painting.

We have an hour to wander through the rooms; me, enjoying myself and forgetting to talk to the pupils. But they are all fifteen, rising sixteen; they can look after themselves. The warden follows at an indiscreet distance, the list of 'no's' dancing in his head.

I leave Mrs Gerard and Mr Pretty discussing *Figure Standing* and skive off down the corridor. I creep into a white room which has pictures of harbours and people. There is a woman with a yellow and purple face, disconnected teeth and one enormous green eye.

> *When shown this picture*
> *Mme Lefèvre's daughter*
> *gave a shout of recognition*
> *crying Mama*

There are whirls of colour in this room. I could sit here on this couch and look at them until the gallery closes. Perhaps they will forget about me and go home on the bus, chewing toffee, being forced to listen to 'Fanfare for the Common Man.' It is quiet in here, and clean and cool, with a thermostat that ticks. No-one seems to like this room. No-one comes in.

Mrs Gerard finds me though.

'Oh,' she says. 'Are you all right?'

'Fine,' I say.

But it is not all right to sit here. Mrs Gerard stands next to the woman with the disconnected teeth and tells me off. I should be chaperoning, shepherding, pointing things out. This is not a teacher's holiday, she says, this is a responsible position. So I get up blushing, and scuttle to look for my sheep.

Michael Douglas's group are standing round a metal sculpture called 'Woman with her Throat Cut.' I don't feel they need protection.

Graham the serious boy is standing by himself, looking at a picture of a fish on a table.

'Do you like this picture, Graham?' I ask him.

'John,' he says. Damn. I always get his name wrong.

'Well,' says John, 'the scales are very well done.'

'Yes,' I say, 'very life-like.'

We stare at it for a while, breathing quietly at a respectful distance. The scales remind me of biology lessons – the little silvery flakes are very accurate. But I don't like it; it is too much like the real thing and I can't help thinking about the taps in the lab. John, though, John seems to want to remain with the fish picture. I feel that I am disturbing him. He ignores me politely and after a while I slink off again and stare chronologically along the walls. There is Cubism and Futurism, but I don't know much about them. One of the fifth-form girls asks me about Cubism.

'I think it's a style of painting that was reduced to a sort of cube representation,' I say, helpfully. 'If you stand back from this picture, you can see that these blocks are actually people.'

The girl stands back and says, 'Oh yes,' and calls her friends over. Perhaps she will remember me for this, not for all the lessons about osmosis and semi-permeable membranes. Perhaps one day she'll say, 'My biology teacher was the first person to explain Cubism to me.'

Twenty minutes come and go in this room. The cubes get to me after a while; they seem to accuse me of something, of a lack of comprehension. Mrs Gerard and Mr Pretty are nowhere to be seen.

'Have you seen Mrs Gerard or Mr Pretty?' I ask one of the girls and she tells me that they are in Room 12. They are looking at the Russian Avant-Garde, she says.

On my way to Room 12 I catch Michael Douglas and Kim Dunn sloping down to the café. There is a blackboard that says Café Open 10–4.30. Morning Coffee. Lunches. Afternoon Tea. 'Off for a morning coffee then, are you?' I say in the voice that is sarcastic; the one that is creaking and unromantic, like the wicked witch of the east. It always surprises me that I speak at all, that I don't just vaporise, like ether, as soon as I walk into school. Kim and Michael shuffle, kicking the rubber tread on the stairs, and mutter about having been through all the rooms already, and it is only eleven o'clock. Kim sways her shoulder bag from one hip to the other.

Well I'm not about to get in the way of true love, etc. so I say I will accompany them down the stairs to check that there's no one else skiving off. Then they can have an uninterrupted coffee for fifteen minutes. But I'll be back, I croak, like that horrible old witch. I'm keeping an eye on you.

We trot chastely down the stairs. It is still raining outside, drizzle flicking onto the window, and the grounds of the gallery are a very beautiful green and some pupils are sitting on the steps eating biscuits.

My colleagues and I are not doing a very good chaperoning job, evidently, but no-one cares. I can see two magpies sitting on the elbows of the reclining woman.

'Look,' I shriek, 'two for joy,' and Kim and Michael turn their heads and look at me.

I change the subject.

'So what have you learned about Cubism?' I ask briskly.

'Nothing at all,' says Michael. 'We thought Mrs Gerard was going to tell us but she seems to have disappeared.'

'Yes,' says Kim. They both frown. Somehow they seem older than me. Kim looks collected in a blue silk shirt.

Wafts of scone and cheese meet us at the bottom of the stairs and I am tempted to forget about my truant count, buy a coffee and just sit there staring out of the window at damp hydrangeas. The café is nearly empty of pupils, but I begin searching anyway, as instructed by Mrs Gerard, searching for possible difficulties, when I hear Michael say, 'Look,' and we are suddenly all staring at them – Mrs Gerard and Mr Pretty – who are quickly disengaging hands at a corner table. They pretend they have not seen us, and from this distance Mrs Gerard looks like the painting of Mme Lefèvre, a strange colour with a sideways-looking eye.

When shown this picture
She gave a shout of recognition
Crying

The cafe chairs make a terrible noise in here but I don't really notice this, I just stand next to a rubber plant and stare. Michael and Kim have already disappeared, they are upstairs telling their friends, leaving me to stare at my colleagues, who just sit there, blushing, blushing and pounding cake crumbs. They are pretending, of course, that this is a figment of my imagination; I'm sure they think if they sit there for long enough, sideways-on, discussing art, I will forget what I saw. But this picture is too simple to forget, too good to be a bad thing.

True If Destroyed

T HE ROOM SMELLED of something; she couldn't tell if it was freesias or cigar smoke. It had a sweet, heavy smell. Mr Müller was standing in front of the mantelpiece, winding up the white hairs on his violin bow. Behind him there were pictures of tiny saints in frames.

'When you are ready, Catherine,' he said.

She could see herself in a long, dark mirror, lifting the violin and putting it under her chin. Her face was a white triangle, the same as it was in department store windows. She breathed and attached her fingers to the strings. She began to play but it felt as if she was floating, silently, somewhere above Mr Müller's piano. It was difficult to hear any music. The room was greyish, pinkish, beautiful, full of things that had been dusted. A sitar was propped against the wall, and ivies hung from bookshelves. There was a low table; people like Mr Müller always had low tables with things on them like Moroccan pottery. Mr Müller was looking through the window at the grey garden, and snorting streams of air out through his nose.

'You are phlegmatic,' he said when she had finished playing. 'There are four types,' he said, 'choleric, melancholic, sanguine, phlegmatic. You are phlegmatic.'

Mr Müller had a very large head that was creased in places, along the edges of his mouth and between his eyebrows. His eyes appeared small behind his glasses.

Catherine said, 'What does phlegmatic mean?' but he was

talking again and didn't answer. One of the framed saints looked just like him, except it was wearing a kind of turban. After a while Mr Müller pulled his lips together.

'Would you like a coffee?' he said.

Catherine's old teacher had never offered her coffee.

'I think we need some refreshment,' he said. 'It is eleven o'clock.'

'Right,' said Catherine, and her voice clanged across the room, like a cow-bell. It made Mr Müller's pottery seem more delicate, as if it might shatter.

'These workmen,' said Mr Müller, twitching the curtains and staring at two men who were hitting the roof of the house opposite with hammers. 'It is impossible to play Bach when there are such people on the roof.'

They went into the kitchen, where a woman was standing at the sink.

'This is Elsa,' said Mr Müller.

Elsa smiled. She was peeling vegetables.

'Elsa is making lunch,' said Mr Müller, unnecessarily. He put his hand briefly on her shoulder, then switched the kettle on. The kitchen was quiet and made Catherine want to stay in it. There was a view onto wide drying greens and chestnut trees. It was so nice around here. Catherine stood near the window and watched toddlers on tricycles, playing around the washing poles. The Müllers' flat was on the fourth floor and she could see all the drying greens in the area, big, emerald and solitary, divided like a baby's jigsaw puzzle. This was a part of town where no-one shrieked or dropped litter. There was a WRVS shop on the corner full of women wearing knee-length skirts. People stood with trowels in their front gardens, poking around the roots of hydrangeas and throwing gravel about. They looked up benignly when Catherine walked past. On the corner of the street, a haberdasher sold linen buttons and hooks and eyes.

Mr Müller made a small amount of bitter coffee and poured it into tiny cups. He got a noisy packet of honeycakes out of the cupboard and opened it. He put seven honeycakes on a large saucer and offered them to her. For a while they chewed and gulped in silence. Catherine hung onto a smile and looked at the things on the Müllers' sideboards. Herbal tea, packets of black seaweed, jars of dried beans and something that looked like a wooden rhino that was nodding its head, very slightly, in the draught. The saucepan on the cooker was making noises and occasionally flinging a red mixure onto the floor tiles. 'The soup looks intriguing,' Catherine said. Elsa was hurling everything into it: vegetables, spices, meat, sugar.

'How old are you, Catherine?' said Mr Müller. He had his head on one side and was looking at her as if she was a natural curiosity; some strangely shaped pebble. Elsa made a sniffing noise and continued to peel parsnips.

'I'm fourteen,' said Catherine.

'Ah,' said Mr Müller. 'Just the age for being phlegmatic.'

'You're being *enig*matic, my darling,' said Elsa, and they both laughed with their mouths wide open, as if this was the funniest joke. Catherine licked honey from the corners of her lips and felt the beginning of a stomach ache. It was too late now to ask what phlegmatic meant.

There was a boy at school called Craig Morris. He and Catherine used to cross paths every Tuesday, just by the delicatessen; to avoid him would have involved a twenty-minute detour. They walked past each other in silence, avoiding eye contact. People at school assumed that they were in love because they both owned violins. 'I bet they play duets,' said a girl called Mandy Boyle. 'They have the same initials,' she said. Mandy Boyle always seemed to have green ink on her hands and sometimes she stabbed herself with compasses to see how much it hurt. Her friends clung to her fearfully. In the October whiteness of bus windows she wrote:

CM 4 CM. (True If Destroyed, True If Not Destroyed)

It made Catherine think of the way people used to throw witches into rivers; you were innocent if you drowned, guilty if you survived.

There were a lot of unusual people at school; there was a girl called Cindy Button who had no eyelashes and a boy in the sixth form who smelled of sweat and everyone said had gland problems. Craig Morris looked pretty normal although he never combed his hair and his clothes hung at awkward angles. The worst thing was to be paired up with him in class, which happened a lot. The teachers also seemed to think it was touching that they both played the violin. 'Catherine remains a little unworldly,' her last report card had said. Maybe it said the same on Craig's.

One afternoon they had to dissect things and Catherine told the teacher she did not want to be paired up with Craig again, so he sat by himself with a dead fish, surrounded by four feet of nothing. Catherine was paired up with Cindy Button instead. 'Hi, Cathy,' Cindy said, in her high voice. Pale pink blood ran along a newspaper-wrapped trout.

'How are your violin lessons going, Cathy?' she said. She blinked and Catherine thought of baby mice.

'OK,' said Catherine. 'My teacher's a funny bloke though. We spend half the time drinking coffee.'

'Maybe he fancies you,' said Cindy, and Catherine noticed a slight change in the way Craig was sitting at the bench in front of them; a strange re-positioning of his head that made her think he was listening.

'I don't think so, Cindy,' said Catherine. 'I think he just likes drinking coffee.'

The smell of trout was making her feel unwell. She tried not to look at it, at the way one blank eye fixed its stare on the ceiling. Cindy picked the trout up and some of its scales stayed behind on the wooden table. They were transparent, like tiny fingernails.

'My dad said to bring it back for supper,' said Cindy.

'Oh God,' said Catherine. She remembered that her mother had once pulled out a set of eyelashes by mistake, with eyelash curlers. They took about two months to grow back.

They had a piano at home but it was not as delicate as the Müllers'. It had scrolls and spirals all over it, like some sea creature. Mr Müller used to phone up every few months and ask Catherine to play middle C down the receiver. 'Hmm,' said

Mr Müller, and he would hit middle C on his own piano, in his distant living room on the other side of the city. 'That sounds about right,' he said. Catherine would twist the phone wire twice, three times around her finger and try to picture everything in Mr Müller's sitting room.

The Müllers' entrance hall had Peruvian wall-hangings and a walnut chest of drawers. There were photographs on it of their children; young men with beards. It was strange that people with beards could still be called children. Mr Müller mentioned them occasionally. One of them was an architect in New York and the other one was working in Andalucia. 'We got a letter from David this morning,' said Mr Müller. 'At the moment, he is extracting honey.'

Catherine was not sure where Andalucia was exactly.

'What do you want to do when you leave school?' Mr Müller asked.

'I don't know,' said Catherine. 'I won't be leaving for another four years yet.'

'Four years,' said Mr Müller. 'When you are old, a whole *year* is like four weeks.'

After the lesson, Elsa sometimes brought coffee into the living room, with a plate of star-shaped shortbread.

'Elsa is composing a symphony,' said Mr Müller.

'Really?' said Catherine. The shortbread collapsed when she bit it, and landed on the carpet.

'Catherine is playing very well,' said Mr Müller to Elsa.

'I heard,' said Elsa. 'It sounded beautiful.'

'The fast bit is quite tricky,' Catherine said, because she had to say something. Elsa was looking at Mr Müller with a sad smile that she did not understand. She wanted to ask Elsa about her symphony, but it was difficult to know what to say; the Müllers left her speechless. They composed music and they were also composed; they seemed to glide a few inches above the floor, touching things gently and smiling and humming. If you gave them a Ming vase they would hold it firmly even though it looked as if they were about to drop it. Catherine dug little dents into her thumbs with her index fingers. The wicker of her chair squeaked and she looked down at the bowl of shortbread. Each piece was covered perfectly in vanilla sugar.

'Would you like another one, Catherine?' Elsa said, picking up the bowl and moving it nearer.

During the Easter holiday her mother bought her a pale green bra and in the summer term she was gathered up, suddenly, by the trendy girls, like part of a sparkling shoal of fish. They just zoomed in from somewhere and snapped her up. She watched Cindy Button receding into the dark corners, the murky green angles of the changing room, like a piece of seaweed, waving sadly.

'Are you coming to Chez Moi on Friday?' said Mandy Boyle. She pronounced it Chezz Moy, because that was ironic. Chezz Moy was at the grey, the raining end of town, at the back of the station, between a carpet warehouse and something Mandy called a 'dodgy lingerie shop,' that had bendy felt models in the windows which wore pink suspender belts and matching camisoles. People said it was run by an Italian called Giuseppe who couldn't keep his hands off you. Giuseppe, they said, was very quick at removing your bra. 'You ought to go to Chezz, though,' said Mandy. Sometimes, when Mandy spoke for a long time, she had to close her eyes in order to be able to work out her next sentence.

'I might,' Catherine said. Since she had started wearing a bra, life seemed tight and uncomfortable. Everything loomed and felt desolate; she would stand on the netball pitch wearing an orange tunic that said WING and she would want to cry. The despair in people's voices wailing, 'To me, Cathy, pass it,' made her ache and want to evaporate. She hated being called Cathy. It was always windy and cold and people's legs were mottled like salami, and none of it mattered. Sometimes she felt that she was about to be sick.

Mandy Boyle spent a couple of weeks choosing a new hairstyle for Catherine. She brought a magazine called *Hair* into school, and circled pictures of transfixed-looking women. 'You should get it cut like that,' she said. 'You would look quite pretty if you had it flicked'.

'I hate flicked hairstyles,' said Catherine, and Mandy stood close to her, breathing 'Do you?' Do you?' At night, Catherine began to have nightmares about monsters and things chasing her. She dreamed that the models in the lingerie shop had come to life, had become massive in size and were pursuing her in their camisoles down the highstreet.

'We must postpone our next lesson,' said Mr Müller. He phoned her on Sunday evening, when she had nothing to do, when she was lying on the floor and wondering if she would ever experience an interesting Sunday. 'You could read,' her mother always said, 'or go for a walk. Or write letters,' and every suggestion made Catherine feel more hopeless. 'I am not well,' said Mr Müller's voice on the phone, and he described the way he was feeling, as if she was not a child. He did not talk to her the way most adults did. He told her he was sweating and tired. 'My limbs are heavy,' he said, and he talked as if he was analysing someone else.

'It sounds like flu,' said Catherine, and she twisted the telephone wire twice, three times, around her little finger. She imagined his face at the other end of the line, a big, soft face like one of the saints in the pictures. Mr Müller practised meditation and something called the Alexander Technique; there was a little room in his flat that he used for this. It had a stripey rug and candles and always a vase of fresh flowers.

'Yes,' said Mr Müller, 'I am ill.'

'Well,' said Catherine, 'I hope you get better soon.'

She sent him a postcard. A picture of a sailing ship, with a gold and blue sky.

'Sorry to hear you are not well,' she wrote. 'Get better soon,' and she felt old and sensible, like her mother. Possibly phlegmatic; she felt it might mean something like that.

The doorman at Chez Moi was perfectly oblong, like a loaf of bread. He grabbed Catherine's wrist when she got to the front of the queue and slammed a stamp on it. The print was invisible until she stood under the dance-floor lights, and then it was revealed, a purple X. Mandy had brushed her teeth with Pearl Drops to make them look extra-white, and when she smiled under the strobe lighting, her mouth lit up like a torch. 'Wow,' said her mouth. 'The stripes in your trousers are bizarre.' Catherine did not reply. Once they had left their coats at the cloakroom, Mandy took charge. She told Catherine what to do and guided her around the club, prodding her occasionally in the back when she seemed to be going in the wrong direction. At the bar, she asked for two Barcardi and Cokes and a packet of nik-naks.

'How old are you?' asked the bar-tender, stroking his stubble.

'Eighteen,' said Mandy.

'And I'm Raquel Welch,' said the bar-tender. They returned with their packet of nik-naks to a small round table.

'There's your admirer,' said Mandy. Catherine turned in her chair and saw Craig Morris, standing with a friend beside a swirling orange poster. He looked as if he was concentrating extremely hard on a conversation and his clothes were still too big for him, and too homely for Chez Moi.

'What's he doing here?' Catherine said, putting on her strange Mandy-voice.

'He's quite good-looking actually,' said Mandy, 'Now he's got his hair cut.'

They walked into the middle of the dance floor and danced. Mandy had a peculiar style, as if someone had put a lot of starch in her clothes. She had a repertoire of three moves; one: a pummelling motion with the wrists, two: shifting her weight from one foot to the other, three: turning round. Sometimes she held her head back, shut her eyes and mimed the words. Every time Catherine looked at her watch, the time still seemed to be 10.36.

'I'm just off to the loo,' Catherine shouted into Mandy's ear. She had to get away.

'Shall I come?' said Mandy, staring at her. 'Shall I come?'

'No,' said Catherine, 'I think I'll be OK.'

The last time she saw Mr Müller, he told her about an article he had read in the paper, about some pigeons that had been

60

dyed different colours. Someone in London had grabbed these pigeons on April Fool's Day and dyed them blue, pink and orange. Then they had released them. At first, people thought they were a kind of large canary.

'People are curious,' said Mr Müller, winding the hairs on his violin bow, shutting the window so the clangs from the workmen were a little less. 'But they must have looked fine, actually.' That afternoon they ate apricot cake with Elsa, and sat in an oblong of sunlight that illuminated tiny flecks of dust. The room was greyish, pinkish, beautiful.

Craig Morris phoned, a week later, first to ask her out and then to tell her that Mr Müller had died, that he had been very ill, didn't she know that? and that was what she had thought of first, even before she put the phone down, even before she could believe she would not see him again; the taste of apricot and the sunlight and the conversation about coloured pigeons. She wanted to separate that afternoon from all the others, all the sad, strangling days. She just wanted to hold on to it.

Barettes

M Y MOTHER LOOKS tired. She sits on one of the Jobcentre's tweedy seats and looks in her bag for a biro. Then she walks over to the catering adverts and scans the board.

Today they are playing Beethoven's Ninth. Everyone is going through adverts for sporran makers and panel bashers, and there's this triumphant singing. Perhaps there is some kind of psychology behind it. Music to inspire; music to make you think you want to be a panel basher. Or perhaps there is no psychology. My mother and I sign on on the same day, Wednesdays at 3 o'clock. You'd have thought we'd be split up, being family, in case we did something illegal; lie about something. But they haven't separated us yet.

My mother used to be a cook at a primary school, one of those cooks the children liked. There is always one they like and one they hate, it's just the way it is. The one they hated was called Mrs Marvel, and she had tight orange curls and things she stuck into them called barettes. She used to smash her ladle against the counter and shout Silence, like one of the teachers, and when she opened her mouth her teeth were blue-brown from nicotine. Mum crept in the background, behind the serving hatch, trying to knock lumps out of the potatoes.

Now I can hear her sighing, and she writes down a reference number. I should be looking too, but lethargy grips me. I push myself into the upholstery and try not breathing. The room is blueish. On the wall is the jobcentre sign: a circular picture of a man changing colour as he walks through a door. Unemployment is symbolised by the colour yellow. But it's not like it used to be. There are plants here these days and you get printed slips to write your reference numbers on. The metal strips on the advert boards make it look Art Deco-ish, elegant. Yes we all look very elegant nowadays, very noble, and people hardly ever throw up.

After a bit a girl in a transparent blouse calls out, 'Mrs Moore.' That's me. I get up and go over to the desk with my green book. This never takes long. The more ignorant you look the quicker it takes, so I always have my dumb expression. The girl looks about sixteen, unwrinkled, unspotty. I am going through a wrinkled, spotty stage. It is not fair to have both. One or the other, but not both.

'Hallo,' says the girl.

She gets out the bit of paper. My signatures line up on it like thin insects and I am always surprised that they still mean something, that I don't just have to press my thumbs against a computer screen.

'I see you've been out of work nearly six months now,' says the girl, looking at her notes. Staff are wily these days; I wonder if they are bugged. The girl is wearing varnish on well-cut nails that rise up a bit in the middle, the way they're supposed to. Her fingers shake a little as she points out the place I have to sign.

My mother has always been more careful than me. She reads everything before she signs it, puts documents away in drawers where she knows she'll find them. At cash points, she stabs the numbers slowly and always gets a receipt. I am aware of her smiling and clearing her throat at the desk next to mine, then she signs and nods, picks up her bag and turns away.

I meet her at the exit. 'See anything?' I ask her. She shakes her head and says, 'I'd like to visit the Ladies.' I think she must be the only person here who would say something like that. Even the door does not say 'Ladies.' It just indicates that people with one leg and a triangular skirt can go in. There is one free cubicle. Mum goes in first then I go in while she washes her hands.

The walls are jumping with graffiti. A little circle of paper has been torn off at eye level, and someone has written in the circle, 'I'm pink therefore I'm Spam.' The rest of it is mainly Sally 4 James Ferguson. No anatomical drawings, but that's what men do. This is quite intellectual stuff.

At the basin, my mother examines her hair, the bags under her eyes. I only notice her aging sometimes. Usually she looks about the age she was when I was ten. 'God, I need a haircut,' she says. 'Or maybe I should get some barettes like Mrs Marvel's.' And she laughs the way she always does, nearly crying because the thought of Mrs Marvel in barettes is so strange. She laughs. I come here every fortnight and afterwards I just feel like sitting in a bath for the rest of my life, floating in soap bubbles. But my mother laughs. She makes plans, takes out her list and reads the things we have to do.

'Lightbulbs,' she says. 'Toothpaste. Shoes to be re-heeled.'

I look down and wash my hands.

Broadcast

THE POETS WERE sitting in a roped-off section of the room. Some were famous. Others were described as 'fresh and new,' as if they were asparagus tips or clean bed-linen. Mary's husband was sitting amongst them looking old, his hair as white as cuttlefish.

Five microphones stood on the floor. 'Why do you think there are so many of those things, dear?' Mary heard someone say, and something about the question made her lonely. She wanted to be sitting there with someone, calling them 'dear' and talking about the shapes of things. Just to be perched there, alone in the front row with her mouth shut, embarrassed her. She tried to catch her husband's eye but he wasn't looking; he was just there in his new shoes, with poetry books on his lap. Above his head was a pattern of coloured glass and it made Mary think of chapels, as if everyone was sitting there waiting for forgiveness. Someone said, 'That's David Michaels,' and when Mary heard his name she could feel herself blush.

Another day kept coming into her mind. It was the sky that had reminded her; the way it looked endlessly blue and thick, as if you could stir it with a spoon. She had been drawing a picture of the primroses in her window box, breathing in the sugary smell of them, when he had appeared on the pavement outside, wearing a hat. She had thought the hat looked ridiculous; it was a straw hat – too big for him, and it didn't suit his face. He always behaved as if he lived in Florence, not Merchiston. As soon as the sun came out he turned brown and started buying Italian loaves and mortadella.

'Let's go for a walk,' he said. They had known each other for six weeks. His undisguised interest in her made her smile.

They drove to the beach in his car. The car was full of stuff; chocolate wrappers and bits of metal and plastic and tin cans. In the glove box there were pieces of paper with writing on, poems maybe. She read the corner of one that began 'Leave me alone' but she couldn't make out the rest of it. There were also tea-stained books and very old grey sweets and the rose of a watering can under her feet. She was young and excited at the time and thought that all these things had meaning; that they said something about his soul. They went for a long walk along the edge of the sea and he picked up bits of shellfish and found metaphors for them. She laughed when his hat blew away and went scudding off into the waves, but he took it very seriously. That was the first time she heard him swear, in a young, high voice. Everybody said he was talented and slightly odd and this was very attractive.

They got back into the car and drove to a tea-shop. It was in a big red municipal building that overlooked the sea. To Mary it seemed rather gloomy but David said it was a fine example of Victorian architecture. Also, they did toasted teacakes. While they ate, David grieved for his hat. 'It was a fine hat,' he said. 'I only had it for three days.'

'Maybe it was meant to happen,' said Mary. 'Maybe someone on the other side of the Atlantic will pick it out of the sea.'

'I think not,' said David, putting teacake into his mouth and picking up his cup of hot chocolate. Mary thought he did not have a very poetic attitude about his hat; she thought he would have understood about freedom and spontaneity and things having their own soul.

After a while David seemed to relax. The hot chocolate tasted good and he told her that somebody had just accepted some of his poems.

'They are a sequence about chimneys,' he said.

Mary had never heard about sequences of poems before.

'What do you say about these chimneys?' she asked, but David said she would have to read them.

'There's no point talking about them,' he said.

'But you are,' said Mary.

'Yes, but,' said David, then he stopped talking. His face became long and melancholy and he looked through the window. The tea-shop was three floors up and there was a pigeon standing on the other side of the window, looking back at him. The pigeon had a scrappy little nest, made from bits of straw and ice-cream wrappers.

'Ah,' said David, 'look at that,' and he smiled, as if all his anxieties had disappeared. This was what fascinated Mary; the way his moods changed his face, as if someone kept chalking his expression on and then wiping it clean.

David became famous gradually. It was like growing up with royalty. Critics began to write reviews of his work, and paragraphs for his book-jackets; they composed sentences about 'the pure line of his verse' and 'his crystal-clear melodies.' People called him the leading poet of his generation and wondered how he managed to write so prolifically. Actually he had a number of methods: sometimes he went on solitary holidays without warning; sometimes he stayed up all night, smoking Gitanes with an anguished expression; sometimes he wrote random words down on pieces of paper, or cut them out of newspapers, then connected them all together. 'Isn't that cheating?' said Mary.

'There is no correct way of writing a poem,' said David. 'Words lead to more words.' Sometimes he was silent for days.

He occasionally wrote about Mary, pretending that these poems were not about her at all, but about womankind. 'They are universal, darling,' he said, amazed at her paranoia, but she could recognise herself. He included little give-aways; descriptions of her hairstyle, or her habit of losing keys and hairbrushes. One poem, entitled *Woman and Home*, began:

The perplexing wisdom of her eyes
Behind those convex lenses
Sees further than the lie
Of the land . . .

'Why don't you ever *say* things like that?' Mary said, as they ate breakfast one morning. 'Why do you have to write it down first and get it published?'

'What do you mean?' said David, and he looked a little self-conscious as he sprinkled a thick layer of sugar on his rice crispies. This was what he had eaten at breakfast for the past thirty-six years, since they had first started living together. They had reared their children on rice crispies and strong coffee.

'Well,' said Mary, getting up and moving things off the table, 'they're concave anyway.'

She loved disconcerting him. She could always see exactly what he was doing, even when he thought he was being very discreet. She washed up the rice crispie bowls and wondered what her life would have been like if he had not turned up that morning when she had been drawing primroses. She might not have been a part of arguments about poetry and domesticity, about how the two of them were incompatible. Maybe she would have become famous herself, a famous painter, instead of having a lot of paintings in plans chests and sketch-books. Maybe she would not have found herself crying sometimes, when he drove off, in a series of shinier cars over the years, but in the same poetic rage. Occasionally she thought about the hat, sailing away on the Atlantic, like a straw boat.

Because it was a recording studio everyone was scared into silence, hardly daring to pick up a handkerchief or to put a cough sweet in their mouths. At ten thirty a door opened. A short woman wearing headphones walked quickly towards the interviewing table and sat down. She said her name was Barabara Rose, and she talked about a veritable array of talent on the podium tonight.

'Ha!' said a woman in a balaclava. 'They always say that!'

Barbara Rose seemed to hear her, even through her foam-rubber headset. She turned slightly and fixed her small round eyes on the woman.

'First,' she continued, smiling again, having established her authority, 'and arguably the finest writer of his generation . . .'

And Mary wondered why announcers always seemed to put *arguably* in front of everything. No-one in this audience was likely to argue, apart from, perhaps, the balaclava woman. She looked at David and saw his hands shaking as they held his poetry books. She could not remember him looking nervous before; he usually leaped up from his seat and began to read at once, with no introduction. He did not behave like most seventy-three-year-olds.

'. . . and without further ado . . .' said the woman at last, and David stood up. Mary saw his hands shaking and she felt dizzy; she was not breathing deeply enough. She looked at her own hands, clutched tightly together like a boxer's gloves. When she looked at David again, something about the way he was standing there in his new shoes made her want to rush up and wrap her arms around him. The beige lace-ups looked so clean, not worn enough to venture into a poetry reading. They were like him; they had a label inside them that said *Rugged* but it didn't suit them. Mary felt strange, to be the only person in the audience who knew anything about these shoes, when the audience had learned so much about her, over the years. David had galloped home from the shoe-shop, excited, with the shoes already on his feet. 'They're called Rugged,' he said. The name seemed to be what appealed to him most. Mary felt some stupid tears in her eyes. It was strange how much love you could feel for a person's clothes; for their reasons for wearing them.

'I only came here to hear David Michaels,' she heard someone say, and she felt the way she always did at his poetry readings; as if someone had taken something away from her that had never really been hers.

David walked up to the maraca-shaped microphone. 'I should be shaking this, not reciting poetry into it,' he said. There

69

was a short silence, and then everyone laughed. David always charmed his audience. Seeing similarities between things was a useful social skill; also a kind of nervous twitch. The woman in the balaclava laughed, clapped her hands together and then stopped.

A red light-bulb went on above David's head, like an idea in a cartoon. 'Right,' he said, shuffling his books into the correct order. Mary closed her eyes for a moment and he still sounded thirty-two. Sometimes, when they arranged to meet in town, outside Frasers or Jenners, she found herself looking out for a young man with dark hair and a suede jacket.

As David began to read, she looked at the churchy glass panels. There were four colours: red, blue, green and gold. If she creased her eyes up, the colours began to merge and form shapes, like strange paintings. She didn't have her glasses on. David read that one to start with, the one about her convex lenses. It was one of his favourites; he read it out so often that he had disassociated himself from it. It wasn't about him and Mary any more; it was like a shape in the snow, when the person who made it has got up and walked away. Everyone sighed when he finished it. David could make a whole audience hold its breath. With every poem, he became more confident; his hands stopped shaking and his voice rose until the whole room was filled with metaphors. For a while he shuffled through some of his 'lighter' repertoire – the one about milking cows as a boy, the one about the man in the estate agents and the one about cats.

'And finally,' he said, 'I'm a little nervous because this is the first time I've read this particular poem to anyone. It is dedicated to my wife and it is called *The Hat*.'

Mary closed her eyes tight, very tight, but her ears were filled with sound. She could almost hear people smiling when he dedicated the poem to her, the way they would smile at something touching, like a kitten or a scene from Pinnochio. The poem was about a young man and woman on a beach, picking up shellfish and laughing as the man's hat was blown away and washed out to sea. David read it calmly and clearly; he included lines about the hat's poetic soul, its sudden bid for freedom. '*Both of them knew this* . . .' he read in a clanging kind of voice, and he described how the young man had thrown his bare head back and laughed.

There was wine after the reading. A crowd of people hung around, fingering their wine-glasses and staring at close range while David described his working day. Mary stood at a distance and listened to them talking about '*The Hat*.'

'I could almost feel the sand under my feet,' the balaclava woman said, and she did not seem so mad any more; just a little infatuated maybe, and flattered that David should have written about something you put on your head.

Mary stood on the linoleum and put her hand up to her mouth. That day, the day of the hat, had been hers, printed plainly inside her own head; and David had taken it from her, twisted it into a shape she did not recognise. It would fade now, like other days. The poem would take over. 'David,' she said. All she could see of him was the toes of his new shoes and the top of his hair, frothy and white under the strip lights. He looked as if he was drowning. 'David,' she said. Part of her wanted to rush in and rescue him, but something was gone already.

How To Shop
In Other Languages

THE WOMAN AT the cheese counter is called Miss McGregor. She puts my quarter of brie on the scales, presses a button and some words appear on a screen. LOOSE BACON.

'Christ O'Reilly,' says Miss McGregor, and she presses another button. The writing flickers away and is replaced by something longer: GET A BETTER CHOICE OF CHEESE AT TESCO. Then LOOSE BACON comes back again.

'It's these wee numbers,' she says.

'Uh-huh,' I say.

Shopping at Tescos is like hallucinating. I stand in this loud space and stare at yellow blocks, at signs that say Orkney Mature and French Goats, and nothing comes into my mind. Not even goats. Not even French goats.

Now Miss McGregor is talking to a spotty man who has a paper hat on. 'They haven't put the right numbers in,' she is saying and the man is getting a pen out of his top pocket and sucking it. I can hear the lid clicking against his teeth. I look away down the supermarket and watch a woman prodding a kipper at the fish counter.

'That everything, love?' Miss McGregor is saying when I turn back. She and the man have got the writing to say LOOSE CHEESE now and they are both smiling across the cheese counter at me. She is wrapping my brie up in a single sheet of clear plastic, sticking the price tag over the fold. I like the way they do that; it looks neat; it looks as if you have really bought something.

'That's it, thanks,' I say, like someone in a text book called *What To Say At Supermarkets*.

Miss McGregor hands me my triangle of brie and returns to the cooked meats.

They have changed the lay-out. There are eggs where there used to be orange juice, and it makes you forget what you came in here for. Maybe that is the point. Maybe it is to make you fill your trolley in panic, with things you don't need. But now I remember there is a list in my bag. I wrote it a few days ago. It says

Kidney beans
Milk
Bleach
Tin tomatoes
Golden syrup

I can't think why I wanted golden syrup or kidney beans. It makes me feel sick and I put it away again.

There is something going on in my head but I can't tell what it is. I really have no excuse; something has just slipped. Today I find that I am floating two inches above the floor, looking at rows of cans from a great distance. Maybe that's what happens when you go to the supermarket too often; maybe your mind just vanishes down one of the aisles. But I am very quiet about it; I hardly disturb the air.

People at work said I needed a break so I have bought a ticket to the Faroe Islands. I want to visit all the places that feature on the Shipping Forecast. So far I have been to Ross and Cromarty. I will be going to the Faroe Islands in a week's time. I have read up about them already, and looked at pictures. There are a lot of pictures of sunsets, very beautiful and mysterious. Underneath there are words like Solsetur av Slaettaratindi, which means the Faroe Midnight Sun. It is very exciting to think that I am going to the Land of the Midnight Sun.

73

Baking Needs. I have no baking needs; I skim into the cereals aisle. Why is it that cereal packets are yellow and have pictures of animals on them? One of them has a rhinoceros on the front so I put that in my trolley. Then I put a bag of oats in there, a packet of Rice crispies, a packet of Weetabix, a box of Multi-Cheerios and a bag of muesli. My family likes cereal. My trolley has the ubiquitous dodgy wheel of course. It gambols ahead of me, attracted to Daddy's Sauce and Pickled Vegetables. It is hard not to crash.

The supermarket is full of old men with tins of meaty chunks in gravy for themselves and their dogs. We all wander slowly, companionably, occasionally looking up and manoeuvring our wheels past each other. I think I am the only person in here who is not an old man. I don't know how long I have been here. Maybe an hour and a half. The aisles are full of things that bewitch, things that jump into your trolley. Pilsbury Doughboy Croissant Mixture. French Breakfast Blend Coffee. If you buy enough of this stuff maybe you will turn into someone who bakes and eats croissants with a handsome lover; maybe you will turn into someone else.

The other day someone else's postcard came through the letterbox; that was a start. It was addressed to a person called Sheila McDonald, which is definitely not my name. The picture was of St Patrick's Church in Glendalough, Ireland. Funnily enough, my husband is called Patrick. The person who wrote the card was called Susan. She said:

Just to let you know we're visiting churches only – definitely no pubs – no Guinness! I know you will believe this of me! Having an easy, relaxing and very enjoyable time! What a great place! See you soon.

Just like me, she uses too many exclamation marks on her postcards home. The printed text at the bottom said that St Patrick founded a monastery in the sixth century which grew into one of Europe's foremost centres of learning. I felt mean that I couldn't pass this information on to the real Sheila McDonald. I felt as if I had stolen something.

The next day we got another card from Susan, this time to

someone called Maggie Clifford. It said *Sending this via Sheila! Can't remember your address!* The card talked about the unique beauty of Ireland's landscape and its rich historic, literary and artistic associations. You can give me that any day, a country rich in history, literature and art. I expect the Faroe Islands have their share of it.

This year Patrick is taking the boys to Florida. I couldn't face it, the thought of all those plastic animal heads, all those nodding Mickeys. Disneyland staff get the sack if they are caught smoking with their Mickey heads on. But the boys are excited. I think Patrick is excited too, pleased that we can go away separately, that we can all split up in a mature way even though the boys are only six and eight. We can compare holiday notes when we get back. Donald Duck versus Rocky Outcrops.

I am fumbling through the frozen peas now. This place is called the chilled cabinet, and it sends out glacial air. Everyone came into the supermarket wearing summer things; shorts and T-shirts, and now they are walking around the chilled cabinets, rubbing their arms. The supermarket should give customers gloves in this aisle. There should be gloves hanging by the side of the freezer, like rolls of plastic bags in the vegetable section. But I suppose they would get stolen. They would disappear.

I am putting my frozen peas inside a plastic bag. This is something you do with frozen things, even though the water drips through anyway. It is one of those things you don't question. Maybe there was a reason for it once. I have everything now: lumps of cheese, tins of baked beans, boxes of fish fingers. Before I shove it all up to the till like some big dust-cart, I put a box of Smarties and a packet of razor blades on top of the pile. For my sons; for my husband.

The tills are like airport customs but none of us can pass the green light.

I locate the one with the smallest queue. I am already in line behind three old men with tins of meaty chunks when there is a rumble of trolley wheels and someone starts shrieking my name. Someone is bearing down on me. I look for a place to hide but there is nowhere; there is just white space. A woman with a stiff haircut is falling towards me. She has an enormous pack of Economy Cheesy Wotsits in her trolley. She is shouting my name but I don't know who she is. I want to say, 'Sorry, wrong number,' the way you do on the phone.

But it is definitely my name.

'Hallo.'

She is elongating the o as if she is really pleased to see me. She has a loud voice and lipstick. People are turning round to look at us and my brain is turning over, trying to think where it has seen the face before. The lines of it are familiar.

'Hallo.' The woman says hallo a number of times and then she stops. She stands there, waiting, and I have to say something. I have to say 'Hi,' with a certain intonation, a tone of recognition.

'Long time no see,' says the woman. Her lipstick is probably called something like Flamingo Pink or Peach Sorbet.

'Yes,' I say. 'How are you?'

'Fine,' says the woman. 'And you?'

'Not bad,' I say. We stand and look at each other, the smiles staying on with difficulty, eventually sliding off our faces altogether.

'How's Patrick?' says the woman. 'And the boys?'

'OK,' I say. 'Off to Disneyland next week.'

'Brilliant,' she says. She has a voice that makes me think of croquet mallets. 'You must be looking forward to that.'

I am trying to see if she has a family by looking at the contents of her trolley. Unless she is a Cheesy Wotsit addict, she probably has children. There is also more evidence: family pack boxes of tea, a nine-pack of toilet roll and a bottle of swampy bubble bath with some ugly plastic toy in there. I hazard a guess.

'How are the folks?' I say.

She tells me the folks are fine. Peter starts school in the autumn. Lucy has lost her first milk tooth.

'You're looking brown,' I say. A strange thing to say to a stranger.

'We've just come back from the south of France,' she says. 'We have friends there,' she says. 'They have an absolutely gorgeous little cottage. Lovely.'

'Yes,' I say. 'Lovely. I got a card from a friend in Ireland,' I say. 'They were having a lovely time too, staying in a cottage near St Patrick's Church.'

'Really?' says the woman. Her face wobbles a little. 'It's not somewhere I've ever been,' she says, 'Ireland.'

'I'm off to the Faroe Islands next week,' I say.

'But I thought you were off to Disneyland,' says the woman. She looks alarmed, as if someone has just built a Disneyland there, too, jutting out into the sea.

I tell her it is just Patrick and the boys who are off to Florida. I am having a holiday by myself. 'I just need a bit of time to myself,' I say, and the woman frowns. She has decided that she does not really want to talk to me any more. Perhaps she has made a mistake. Perhaps it is not me after all.

'Listen,' she says, as if I am not. 'Great to see you,' she says, 'but I've absolutely got to dash. I've got to pick Lucy up in five minutes.'

Five minutes and counting. 'Well,' I say, 'I musn't hold you up. It'll take you a while to get through the check-out with all that stuff.'

She laughs but looks affronted.

'I'll give you a call' she says. 'We can catch up.'

'Yes' I say, but I know she won't. People are such liars.

When I get home I unpack everything. I take the wooden spoons out of a pot and put some beautiful, yellow lilies in there instead. I put Miss McGregor's neat pack of brie in the cheese box and throw all the tins in the cupboard. Then I make myself a cup of tea and sit in the living room. I read Patrick's book: *Teach Yourself Spanish in Fourteen Days*. I doubt if Patrick will need to speak Spanish in Florida but I suppose it is always useful. It is handy to know how to shop in other languages, to know phrases like *Algo Mas* and *Queria un kilo de tomates, por favor*.

I got my P60 today. Confirmation that I don't have to work at the office any more. People who write P60s always seem to have the same kind of hand-writing. Neat, with tricky little curves. There is a section saying

Enter Here

'M' if Male, 'F' if Female

and the 'F' makes me feel like an animal; like something that has been put into a box. You can put your identity so easily in a box. I slide the P60 into my book to mark where I've got to.

Golden State

THE HOTEL ROOM was pink. There was a bed with a pink duvet cover and pillow cases with holes at either end.

'Well,' said John. 'This is quite a room. Look, there's a television.'

He got up onto the bed wearing his shoes, found the remote control and switched the TV on. There was a cartoon involving talking tomatoes. One of them was called Brad. John switched the TV off again.

'America is a strange country,' he said.

Liz picked up a laminated piece of card.

'There is an adult channel,' she said. '*Blue Nights* or *My Secret Life*. You have to pay to be connected.'

She got on the bed. There was a three-foot gap between them, and pink space on either side. From here, when she looked through the window, all she could see was sky. Little strips of grey behind the Venetian blind.

'I didn't imagine California as being so grey,' she said.

'I expect it will get better,' said John. 'There is a swimming pool.'

Having got here, having got off the plane, off the coach, out of the taxi-cab, having finally arrived, there was nothing to do. The room was so full of pink cushions it made her want to cry.

'I'm going to look at the bathroom,' she said, and she swung herself off the bed. The bathroom was pink. It had a low round bath and an industrial-looking shower. There were small pots of things by the basin – honeysuckle shampoo, bubble-bath and Lux soap.

She walked back into the bedroom and went to the window. Outside was the sky, the freeway and concrete buildings. This was The Sunshine State. She had imagined it to glitter.

'What do you suggest I do while you are at lectures?' she said, staring at the sky.

'There's the swimming pool,' said John. 'I think there's a gym somewhere.'

'Oh,' said Liz.

'We are only going to be here for three days,' said John. 'Maybe we can go for some walks when I'm not at lectures.'

'Where can we walk?' said Liz. 'There's just the freeway. There are no fields.'

'It's not my fault,' said John. 'Why do you always make it sound as if it's my fault? I have to be here. We can go to San Francisco on Thursday.'

He got off the bed. 'I'm going to look at the timetable,' he said, and he left the room.

Liz lay on the bed and looked at the ceiling. It was a perfect ceiling. There were no cracks in it, nothing you could make patterns from. The wallpaper was little bunches of flowers and baskets, and if you looked at it a particular way, you could see a face. After a while she went into the bathroom again, took her clothes off and left them on the floor. She worked out how the shower operated, adjusted the temperature. The water pressure was very strong, battering her as if it was some kind of therapy. She noticed that the shower head had some words written on it: *Massage* and *Cascade*. It seemed to be fixed at *Massage*.

There were six towels. She needn't have packed the one from home. These towels were soft and perfumed, and had the hotel's name embroidered in the corner. She stood on one, dried herself with one, wrapped her hair up in one. She opened the suitcase and got out her shorts and a T-shirt, even though it wasn't sunny. She had just begun to comb her hair when she heard the bedroom door open.

'Hallo,' said John, and he came into the bathroom holding a paper bag.

'Hallo,' she said.

'Sorry,' said John, and he put his arms round her. His shirt smelled of washing powder and sweat.

'I thought there would be more to do here,' he said. He gave her the paper bag and she opened it. Inside was a bag of peanuts with a picture of a squirrel on the front.

'I found a shop,' he said. 'It's quite good. They sell things like apples as well.'

'Thanks,' she said. She put the peanuts on the bedside table.

They ate a brown casserole at lunch time. There was a board outside the restaurant which had 'Today's Special' chalked on it. 'Look,' said Liz. 'I wonder what is so special about today.' John didn't seem to hear her. He looked at her, then looked at his watch. Then he walked through a door called 'Conference Venue.' Liz went back to the bedroom, unpacked her own towel from the suitcase and went down to the swimming pool. There were five women lying around the edges, wearing tight gold jewellery.

'Are you a conference widow, honey?' said one of them. Another one flopped over onto her front, making Liz think of seal documentaries. Liz got into her swimsuit, struggling with the straps and legholes underneath the towel.

'Don't be shy,' said one of the women, 'we're all girls together.' Then she squirted a snake of sun tan lotion into her cleavage. 'It's overcast,' she said, 'but that sun is still strong. You should watch that nice white skin.'

'Well,' said Liz, 'I'm just going to swim for a bit.'

She walked to the shallow end and lowered herself into the water. There was a breeze making small blue waves, and she could see goose bumps appearing on the tops of her arms. There was nobody in the pool, but a few ducks had flown in from somewhere and were floating about. Silicon Valley ducks. She could see their legs under the water, much further back then she thought they would be. It was almost glamorous to be swimming with ducks, although swans would have been better, and it occurred to her suddenly that she might be wading around in an enormous duck toilet. She swam ten lengths, keeping her mouth out of the water. There was a black rubber ring floating at the deep end and she leaned against it for a while, letting the breeze dry her skin.

'Look out for those birds, honey,' said one of the women, the one in the black and gold halter-neck.

'Great flapping things,' said another woman, who had a T-shirt with 'Go Surf' written on it.

When she got back to the room she sat on the bed and dried her hair again. Their towel looked strange in this setting, as if it missed the bathroom at home. She hung it over the radiator in the bathroom with the six hotel towels, then she lay on the floor and ate the peanuts John had given her. She found some writing paper and a biro and tried to write a poem. She wrote, *The hotel pool is full of ducks* but she didn't get any further. Writing poetry made her feel hopeless and bitter. She had not imagined she would feel like this in California.

In the evening the programme included something in italics called 'Social.' This was dinner followed by drinks in the *Piano Suite*. Liz found her dress and flattened it as well as she could with the triangular little travel iron they had bought.

At dinner John introduced her to four men. 'Hi,' they said, smiling. One of them said, 'I expect you've been down to the swimming pool.' He looked at her for a while and swivelled some green pasta onto his fork.

'Yes' said Liz, 'there were quite a few ducks in there.'

'Ducks?' said the man and he flipped a twist of the pasta into his mouth. 'Ducks,' he said. 'Well.'

John laughed. Under the table he put his hand on her leg. Liz crossed her legs and his hand moved back again, to settle on his napkin.

'What did you think of this afternoon's lecture, Pete?' he said, and Liz found herself looking away, staring at people on the other side of the room. The pianist had come in and was drinking gin and tonic and rubbing his face. After a while he put his glass on top of the piano and started to play 'Smoke Gets In Your Eyes'. Even from this distance Liz could see how short his hands were. White-skinned and sparkling with signet rings.

'I'm going to sit in one of those armchairs,' she said and John stopped talking and looked at her.

'Are you OK?' he said. 'How about pudding?'

'I don't really feel like pudding,' she said. 'I'll get a coffee at the bar.'

'We'll join you in a minute,' he said and looked at her as if he was trying to communicate something but she let her eyes move away. The four men stopped talking and stared at them.

'Not a bad piano player,' said one of them. 'Worth listening to.' He had a pale circle of red in the white of one eye, lines radiating from it like a cracked windscreen.

Sitting at a table near the piano was one of the swimming pool women. She was wearing a gold dress and gold sandals. Liz could see the creases around the sides of her feet. The woman moved up on the sofa and patted the cushion next to her.

'They play nicely, these pianists,' she said. 'I like watching their fingers.'

'Have you been to many of these things?' said Liz.

'God, thousands,' said the woman. 'My husband is a company director.'

'I see,' said Liz.

The woman rotated her left foot and they both looked at her sandal. Then she picked up her glass and shook the ice around.

'Get out while you can, honey' she said suddenly with her eyes down. 'That's all I have to say.'

She stopped looking at her sandal and watched the piano player again. Liz waited for her to say something else but she didn't seem to want to talk any more. It seemed she had said what she wanted to. The piano player finished 'Smoke Gets In Your Eyes', cracked his fingers and started something else that Liz thought she recognised.

'This is 'Blue Suede Shoes', isn't it?' said the woman after a while. She looked as if she was really trying to work it out.

John had got through nearly a whole bottle of red Californian wine and his breath smelled sweet, the way it does sometimes when people are drunk.

'What was this about ducks?' he said when they got back to the room. He lay on the bed and traced the pattern of the wallpaper with his finger.

'There were about six ducks in the swimming pool,' said Liz. 'I swam around with them for a bit.'

'And who was that woman you were talking to?'

'She said she was a conference widow.'

'Like you,' said John.

He got off the bed and opened his arms but she walked past him into the bathroom. There were seven towels in there now, folded and pink on the radiators. Someone had come in and tidied up while they had been eating.

She realised, suddenly, that the towel from home had also been replaced by a hotel one. She walked out of the bathroom again.

'They've taken our towel,' she said.

John was fiddling around with the blind, trying to get it to close.

'It's supposed to be the other way round, isn't it?' said Liz. 'We're supposed to steal the hotel's towel.'

'Yes,' said John, 'I suppose we are.'

'I liked that towel. I was fond of it,' said Liz. 'It didn't even look like a hotel towel. It had stripes on it.'

'It's just gone off on an adventure,' said John. 'It's gone to check out the American laundry system.'

'I was fond of it,' she said. She remembered the way she had packed the towel at home, thinking of Californian beaches, Yosemite, cable cars. She got into bed and curled her legs up.

John's arms moved around her waist. 'So you went swimming with ducks,' he said, but she pushed him away. She shuffled to the edge of the pink sheet until she was uncomfortable, and stared with her eyes wide open, trying to work things out. The room was stripey because of the light coming through the blinds. John's jacket on the back of the door looked like a strange person. 'In two days' time we'll be in San Francisco,' he said, but she didn't reply. She could hear cars outside. She could imagine truck drivers listening to all-night stations. 'Liz?' said John's voice. After a while she could sense him sleeping, and she put her arms around him, wanting to keep him safe.

Backstroke

MRS LEWIS TAKES ages, whatever she is doing. This is because she is overweight and needs exercise; it's a self-perpetuating thing. 'Slowness makes you overweight, Mother,' says Muriel, 'and that makes you slow.' Now Muriel is waiting for her again, hanging onto the bar at the deep end. The 50+ session has just begun and Muriel is only 35, but no-one is going to haul her out for being fifteen years too young. She'd say that she was there for her mother, anyway; that she was waiting for her mother to get in. She sighs and looks down at her legs. She could have done ten lengths by now. Under the water her legs are lean things, pale as bamboo shoots.

It will be the swimming hat: Mrs Lewis has a swimming hat that will be holding her up. Muriel remembers it from her childhood. It is at least thirty years old, and her mother always has to sprinkle lavender talcum powder into it, then the hat has to be placed on her head just right, not covering her ears but capturing every strand of hair, including the fine hair at the nape of her neck. It has to be just perfect. Muriel tuts: she can't help it. She tuts and stares at the tiles.

Last year Muriel's father died, before she had had a chance to have a two-way conversation with him. She had always imagined a time when they would sit and talk, when they would recline in some green, weed-free garden full of birds, and say quiet, wise things. But he had died and they had never understood each other; there was a little twitch of comprehension, sometimes, but it never lasted. It was hard, that sense of something floating away when you could have grabbed it, hung on to it for a while.

Mrs Lewis talks about him every time they meet, as if she is frightened of letting him go. Her descriptions of him are better than photographs; sometimes, they bring every detail of his face into Muriel's mind. 'Do you remember how he used to balance the washing-up?' she said one evening, and there he was, in Muriel's mind, holding a cup in one hand and a saucepan in the other. 'He used to turn it into a sort of pyramid, do you remember?' said her mother. 'If you moved just one little teaspoon it would have collapsed.' Her mother can get away with sentences like that; she just comes out with them and they are shocking, straightforward as a kiss or a punch. She doesn't seem to know what an effect her words have.

Twice a week they go to a café where Muriel drinks jasmine tea for her nerves and her mother drinks strong coffee and remains calm. Occasionally, they go to watch a matinee at the cinema and Mrs Lewis always takes ages to get ready. She stands in the hallway, behind the cat ornament, and pulls a comb slowly through her hair. 'Is it cold out?' she says. 'Maybe I should wear my coat.'

'No, Mother, it's quite mild,' says Muriel. 'The film begins in fifteen minutes.'

'More haste, less speed,' says her mother, applying lipstick.

Muriel begins to fidget; she picks up pens from the telephone table and puts them down again. She opens the lid of one of Mrs Lewis's many music boxes, winds the key and watches the ballerina turn around. She digs her fingernails into the palms of her hands. 'Just one second,' says her mother, pushing her lips out and inspecting them in the mirror. She is infuriating in the most innocent way, with her quiet voice and her reasonable words. 'You're always in such a rush, dear,' she says. 'There's no hurry.' And they are never late; they walk at Mrs Lewis's pace, heavy as a bassoon solo, and they always have five minutes in which to buy their tickets and a box of chocolates, to go to the WC and to find a seat near the front. 'That's fine,' says Mrs

Lewis, squashing herself into the velvet upholstery, and Muriel wants to hug her there, in the dark; to say sorry. But she doesn't. She never does.

They came out of the cinema one evening and there was a blind man standing at the edge of the pavement, and for the first time in years, Mrs Lewis quickened her pace, almost sprinting along the pavement until she reached him. She wanted to be the first one, of all the people walking past, to help him across the road.

'Excuse me,' she said, out of breath and enthusiastic, 'would you like some help?'

The blind man said that that would be very kind. He took her arm and let her direct him.

'Quite a nice day today,' she said as they walked. 'Sunny.'

'Yes,' said the man, 'quite warm.'

He smiled. He was about sixty, younger than Mrs Lewis. His glasses were so black that you couldn't see his eyes behind them. When they got to the other side, Mrs Lewis stopped, puffing a little after so much exertion, and looked at his face. And Muriel knew she was about to say something bad, something that would make her want to be miles away, down the road, by herself, looking at jars of pickled capers in the delicatessen. Mrs Lewis smiled and cleared her throat. 'I hope you won't take this the wrong way . . .' she said, and Muriel felt her heart constrict, the way it did on these occasions. She could feel her heart coiling up like a snake.

'I've seen you around a lot,' said Mrs Lewis, '. . . and I was wondering if you ever needed a hand, you know, with getting around . . .'

People walking past seemed to slow down a little and stare at them. A baby in a pushchair licked an ice cream and fixed his dark eyes on them. 'Mother,' said Muriel, 'I'm sure . . .'

'That's very kind of you,' said the man to Mrs Lewis. 'My wife normally helps. But that was a very kind offer.'

'A pleasure,' said Mrs Lewis, and she stood and watched, just stood there, overweight in her red coat, as the man clicked away.

'God, Mother,' said Muriel. 'What did you say that for?'

'I thought he might have needed some help,' said Mrs Lewis. 'You know what social services are like these days. I have time on my hands.'

'He was obviously embarrassed,' said Muriel.

'No,' said Mrs Lewis, 'Sometimes you just have to come out and say things. He seems like a nice old man.'

'He's younger than you,' said Muriel. 'He probably thought you were trying to pick him up.'

'Don't be so crude,' said Mrs Louis, and her pale eyes seemed to narrow for a second. 'He still has a wife,' she said, in a quieter voice.

'Blind people must get that kind of thing all the time,' said Muriel. She wanted to be calm and generous but something was always twisting her sentences; being unkind to her mother had become a kind of habit. Spiteful words flew from her just to provoke a reaction, but it never seemed to make any difference – she could say anything she liked and her mother sailed on like a big, double-hulled tanker.

'You don't know how other people feel,' said Mrs Lewis. 'It's impossible to know.'

She hailed a black taxi cab by sticking her fingers in her mouth and whistling. 'I don't see why I should stop doing that just because I'm sixty-seven,' she said. It took her a while to heave herself through the doorway; everything she was wearing and carrying seemed to hold her back. 'Oh,' she said, and she folded her layers of petticoat and skirt and coat beneath her legs and shut the door.

The two old men beside her are discussing floating techniques. 'It's important,' one of them says, 'the way you float. There's an art to it,' he says. He is wearing enormous black swimming trunks.

'Look at Miller,' his friend says in a loud voice. 'He's been in so long he's getting wrinkles.'

Miller looks about eighty-five. He swims very gracefully, dipping his limbs in and out of the water like a newly hatched turtle.

'All right!' the old men say. They push their feet against the wall and swim off in unison. 'Length number ten,' they shout, raising their heads above the water. Muriel tuts. The lifeguard is beginning to pull strings of floats across one side of the pool. Space is being restricted and her mother's not even in yet. Muriel gazes at the turquoise water and wonders what stage her mother is at. But this, generally, is a good thing, she reminds herself, a calming thing, to be here in the pool, waiting for your mother to get in, suspended here like flotsam.

At eleven thirty a pale hand appears round the curtains, and Mrs Lewis stands there, hanging onto two knotted string bags full of clothes and three plastic bottles. Her hat is placed precisely on her head, and the way it flattens her hair makes her look quite triangular. She is wearing the new black swimming costume that Muriel bought her. Size 20.

'Mother,' Muriel shouts, waving and treading water, 'Over here, Mother,' but Mrs Lewis glides past. She walks slowly towards the lockers with her things. She has a 50 pence piece in her hand, which she drops on the wet floor. When she bends to pick it up, she drops her shampoo bottle.

The lifeguard picks it up for her. 'Here you are, dear,' he says and her mother says, 'Thank you. Thank you very much,' in her politest voice. Muriel dips her shoulders further under the water. She is getting cold.

'*There* you are,' Mrs Lewis says, swaying down the steps. 'I didn't see you bobbing about there.'

'I said I'd wait,' says Muriel. She does not like to be described as 'bobbing about.'

'It's not too cold, is it?' says Mrs Lewis, swishing on a huge, happy wave to the edge of the pool.

'I *do* find it cold today actually,' says Muriel. She can feel herself losing control already. 'Maybe because I haven't been moving much,' she says. 'I've just been hanging around.'

'You could have started without me,' says her mother, leaning back against the water and closing her eyes. 'I would have found you.'

Muriel looks away. It is a long time since she has seen her

mother in a swimming costume. She is surprisingly unflabby.
If Muriel didn't swim twice a week and run three times a week,
she dreads to think how flabby she would be.

'This is lovely,' says Mrs Lewis.

'I normally swim forty lengths,' says Muriel.

'Off you go then,' says her mother, and Muriel stares at
her. She can't think what to say; she just treads water like a
peevish duck.

'Aren't you going to swim, too?' she says after a while. 'You
could do with some exercise.'

'In a minute, dear,' says Mrs Lewis.

Benevolent. That is what her mother is. Forgiving.

'Right,' says Muriel. 'I'm doing ten lengths.'

She swims and it seems to take her ages, as if she is pulling her
way through mercury. She gulps water and coughs and has to
stand up for a minute, rubbing her eyes, in the shallow end.
This length has gone wrong and there is nobody to blame, but
she is still angry. She wishes she knew what was wrong with her,
where she got such a temper. When she reaches the edge of the
pool she turns round to look at her mother, but Mrs Lewis is not
there. She was expecting to see her, maybe doing back-stroke like
some big, placid seal but there is no sign of her. Muriel swims
to the steps, stands with the water hugging her waist and feels
suddenly anxious. She pulls herself up the steps and begins to
run along the tiled floor.

'Excuse me,' she says to the lifeguard, 'have you seen a largish
woman in a black swimming costume?'

The lifeguard is wearing a sweatshirt that says 'Raw Energy.'
He looks like the kind of man who might whistle at women,
but not at Muriel, not at Muriel in her wide-strapped swimming
costume. 'A largish woman,' he says, and he smiles. His eyes
move from her chest to an area around her left thigh. 'Well,' he
says, and he tells her he saw a largish woman a minute ago. She
was at the lockers. 'Thanks,' says Muriel, and she walks away,
as dignified as she can, aware of her buttocks.

Her mother is in the shower room. 'Mother,' says Muriel.

She can't believe it. Her mother is just standing there under the water with her eyes shut, and still wearing her swimming costume. She holds her arms up over her breasts, like a shy teenager.

'Mother, what are you doing?' says Muriel. 'I thought something had happened to you.'

Mrs Lewis opens her eyes. 'I just – look,' she says, and she holds out her swimming hat. 'It's perished,' she says. 'I've had it so long and it's perished.'

Under the shower, she looks smaller. 'You were about five when I bought this,' she says.

Muriel takes the hat from her and looks at it. The head-band has come away, forming a sort of handle.

'Oh,' she says.

She slips the hat over her wrist and thinks of Mrs Lewis swimming in it; Mrs Lewis wearing it in a neighbour's pool, summer after summer, teaching her to swim; Mrs Lewis with her dark hair tucked into it. Muriel puts her hand out and touches her white shoulder. 'I'm sorry,' she says. 'I'm really sorry about things.'

'Yes,' says Mrs Lewis.

'Oh,' says Muriel, and she feels ashamed for saying she was overweight, and for the comments about her mother's possessions and her mother's pronouncements, and the way she over-boils rice, and her jingly, jingly collection of music boxes. They really don't matter, they have never mattered, it's just she can't stop herself saying things. 'I'm sorry,' she says, and she looks at the hat again and frowns, trying to think of something funny, something to amuse her mother. 'You could turn it into a fashion accessory – a handbag, look,' she says, swinging the hat from her wrist, but Mrs Lewis just stands there, underneath the shower, and raises her eyebrows.

'Silly girl,' she says, and it feels something like fondness and something like revenge.

Old Women In The Community Centre

THERE ARE EIGHT of us waiting in the hall, underneath the pillars. A production of *South Pacific* had its first performance here last night and there is a painted palm tree on the stage.

The door looks much too small in relation to the pillars. It has a little sticker on it that I can't read from this distance. Probably 'You don't have to be mad to work here but it helps.' The door opens and two women walk through. They have the same coloured hair.

'Hallo,' says one woman. 'My name is Cynthia and this is my mum Cathleen. Mum's just here for the day so don't worry – she'll not be assessing your every move. All right, Mum?'

Cathleen does not say anything and finds a chair. Everyone smiles feebly. We are all sitting on green mats that are crumbling underneath. They look like shredded wheat.

'Now,' says the woman, 'as we're all new to the class I should say a couple of basics about yoga. First, we don't practise yoga in:

trainers

[she marks them off on her hands, bending her fingers back with one long nail]

pumps plimsolls

walking boots

or what have you, so off with all those HORRIBLE shoes and socks.'

She waits for us to pull off the objectionable footwear. There is an elderly man next to me, the only male in the room. When he pulls his socks off he stretches forward and covers his feet with bony hands.

'OK? Wriggle those toes, let the air circulate. Shoes are just boxes that we put our feet in all day. We don't notice, but that's all they are, aren't they? Boxes.'

Cynthia has now taken off her own shoes as well as her jumper, and stands squarely in a black leotard. I feel inappropriate in a pair of elasticated trousers that I bought for a fiver from a sale bin. I painted the hall in them and they are marked with blue flecks. But I notice that no-one else is wearing a leotard either. Everyone looks embarrassed in the wrong kind of clothes.

'Second,' Cynthia says. She speaks too loudly. 'Yoga is not a Doing Thing. It is a Being Thing. It is all about finding your own internal balance. Oh yes, we all have a balance. We just have to find it again. Redistribute ourselves. And if you ever find yourself straining to hold a position, stop IMMEDIATELY. We are very calm in yoga.' Then she starts to jump around, making little shaking movements with her hands.

'Let's get going,' she says, clapping her hands now. 'This is just a warm-up, just to get our bodies working. Shake those feet, wave those arms.'

Everyone limps self-consciously on the mats, improvising a few hops. The woman in front of me has a big body and thin limbs. Apart from me and a girl of about twenty everyone is around retirement age. I look briefly at Cathleen who now sits underneath the palm tree, holding a pair of knitted gloves.

Behind me a woman whispers, 'I thought it was going to be a relaxation class.' Her friend tuts and mumbles.

Cynthia is going to talk us through this. Like 'Music and Mime' broadcasts we had at school. Kids squeaking around the floor in plimsolls while a voice said, 'Quickly, children, find a space and spread out. Remember now – you are a Scared Mouse or a Hungry Cat.'

'We are going to lie flat on our backs,' says Cynthia. 'That's it, find a space, now reach out with those arms making sure you don't hit your neighbour. Not too violent. That's better. Swing those arms, think of a windmill whirring, whirring in the breeze.'

I read once that quite a number of people are actually injured at yoga classes.

While we are lying on the ground waving our arms, a man walks onto the stage carrying a wooden chest. *South Pacific* props.

'Sssh,' Cynthia says and he crouches as if it will make his footsteps quieter, and slinks into the wings. He starts moving chairs around.

'Yoga is best done without external noise,' says Cynthia. 'Isn't that right, James?'

'That's right, Cynthia,' says James's voice from behind the black curtain. We continue waving like daffodils.

But Cynthia suddenly claps her hands again and says, 'Let's move onto a new exercise. If you have a bad back you should not do this one.'

One of the whispering women says, 'That's me out. I had a slipped disc last year.' She sits firmly on her mat, arms crossed, while Cynthia paces in a big circle round the room, instructing us to find some wall. Any bit of flat wall. NO, the radiator will not work. I run around feeling anxious, the last one to find an appropriate space. There are things covering it. Radiators. Coat stand. Unidentifiable metal box. Cast-off shoes. But after a bit we are all hovering in anticipation. Cynthia smiles and says, 'Standing with our BACKS to the wall we slide down onto our bottoms, swivelling ROUND and turning over at the same time TURNING OVER so that we are now lying on the floor with our legs pointing up to the CEILING, all right? It's a very basic position. I have known people sleep like this. No, that's not quite right. Shuffle your bottom nearer the wall. A bit nearer. No.'

Everyone watches while she pulls my legs into position. The blood begins running to my head and when I answer my voice is choked, my chin pressed at a 359-degree angle against my neck.

You are more aware of your bones like this, the combination of bones. Rib-cage and vertebrae. This does not seem a particularly natural position to adopt. My T-shirt struggles but eventually flops over my face and I am aware of everyone turning away discreetly, as if they see strangers' underwear every day.

'OK,' says Cynthia, pleased, and she lets go of my ankles. When I can sit up everyone is already perched, red-faced, on their mats. Ready to fly away.

'All right, Mum?' says Cynthia. Cathleen nods. She has a community centre events programme on her lap.

I had started to notice my bones aching. Yoga seemed the best option. If I sat for more than twenty minutes on a wooden chair, one of my legs refused to work when I stood up. I would scrape it around the house, trying not to bend when I opened cupboards. You never expect to age. You never expect to get lines on your forehead.

Now I can hear everything cracking as we do 'Salute to the Sun.'

'This opens up the whole body,' remarks Cynthia lightly. 'I do this every morning when I get out of bed.'

She lowers her arms as if there are air-bags under them and we try to imitate. She breathes out.

'Haaaaa.'

And her feet make a painful bony sound as she walks across the hall to a large black tape recorder. She switches it on and tries to find the section she wants, re-winding then swearing and fast-forwarding. Uninstructed, everyone begins to mumble shy introductions at mat-level.

'Is this the first time you have done yoga?' I ask the elderly man who has now covered his feet with a jumper.

'It is,' he says. 'I used to do fencing but I gave it up.'

'Fencing?' I can't think what to say. It is hard to imagine.

The two women behind us are lying on their backs again with their legs curled up.

'I like that Salute to the Sun' one of them says. 'I'm going to start doing that in the mornings when I get up. I'm always up early. Seven o'clock most days . . .'

'Are you?' says the other woman. I am aware of her swaying backwards and forwards like a rocking horse.

'I don't think the sun's up by seven at the moment, is it? Not in January. I don't know if you could do a salute to it at seven. I am a hibernator. I don't put a foot out of the bedclothes until nine.'

Voices bounce in the stone hall. From isolated comments to general gossip by the time Cynthia finds the right section. She turns the volume up so we all have to listen. But her voice is suddenly very low.

'We're now moving into the relaxation part of the class,' she whispers. This must be the tone that is used to brain-wash people. Her voice has become featureless, like the music that ripples in one direction then changes its mind and ripples off somewhere else.

'This is the Whispering Willow.'

Her voice is hardly audible. The music tries to form some sort of structure but it can't sustain anything. It is like melting ice-cream. Cynthia tells us to lie down and think of tree roots.

'Mother Earth will bear you,' she says. 'Your legs are two silver streams. Let them flow away.'

I just can't believe that my legs are silver streams. Papier-mâché pineapples roll in the breeze on the stage. In the room next door people have started to clink cups in preparation for the 11 o'clock tea dance. Out of the corner of my eye I can see the man's feet shaking. We are supposed to have our eyes shut but it makes me vulnerable. I like to look at the *South Pacific* set. Somewhere behind the curtains James is still moving chairs but he is trying to be silent. His soles creep.

The women behind me are enjoying this.

'This is nice,' one of them says. 'This is the best bit of the class. I could drop off like this.'

She knocks my head very slightly with her big toe.

'Oops, sorry.'

'Shh,' whispers Cynthia. 'Total quiet.'

So I try shutting my eyes and it does make me less conscious of my elasticated trousers and the women and the bouncing pineapples and the man's feet. The blackness behind my eyes is thick, like soup. People arriving for the tea dance sound very distant, voices dispersed, like listening to a conversation underwater. Cynthia's whispering has faded away but she is still padding about the room, probably checking that we're not peeking. I can hear her ankle crack. One of the radiators clicks like knitting needles. Traffic when the door opens. Silence behind the black curtain. James has gone. I can hear someone saying, 'Where's James? Has he got the key?' but it doesn't impinge at all.

We lie like this for maybe five minutes. I feel incredibly tired, weighted like a soaking duvet. The hall is full of individuals breathing. There are gasping intakes of air on my left and it sounds as if the man is either asleep or concentrating very hard. I have always wanted to know what it is like the second you go from waking to sleeping. Maybe it is like this. Too much effort to think. Letting go. Dark. Dark inside your head and undirected and peaceful at last and

Sudden yellow.

There is a clunking sound and the hall lights are switched on.

The hall lights have been switched on.

Glaring halogen yellow.

'No no,' says Cynthia, running across the hall. Everyone is suddenly on the green mats again, blinking.

'Sorry.'

Cathleen stands in the doorway holding a plate of cakes. She must have crept out while we had our eyes shut.

'I thought it was the tea dance. I just went to help with tea for a bit. I thought you'd be finished.'

'Not for another five minutes, Mum,' says Cynthia, trying hard to be polite. She had got us into this vegetative state and now we are all sitting bolt upright in horror. Everyone looks as if they have had a mild electric shock.

'I thought you were going to the toilet,' says Cynthia. They start talking in low voices in the corner of the room. 'You should have said if you wanted to help with the tea dance. The relaxation is ruined'

98

Cathleen says something about the music on the tape recorder. 'Turning them into old people,' she says. I hear her saying 'Silly,' several times, then 'Mother Earth?' in tones of amazement. She has put the plate of cakes on a chair.

Still sitting on the mat I take off my trousers and stuff them into a Bejam bag. There are no changing rooms here, but as everyone has already seen my underwear it doesn't seem to matter. Most of us are assembled in our coats and anoraks by the time Cynthia is ready to talk to us again. She claps her hands unnecessarily as we have all formed a cluster around her.

'Next week Mum will NOT be here,' she says, giving Cathleen an odd little smile, 'so we can do our relaxation properly. All right?'

Everyone mumbles inconsequentially and shuffles through the small door. I can now see that the sticker says 'Switch Off Lights! Save Electricity!.'

In the hall there is a group of white-haired women in dresses and two thin men waiting for the tea dance. They are making jokes about the cakes on the chair. 'Silver Swan' still ripples away on the tape recorder but it is suddenly snapped off and replaced by

'Any Old Iron? Any Old Iron? Anyanyany Old Iron?'

Cathleen is taking charge, walking quickly in boxy shoes. She smiles at one of the men and places the cakes on the stage. She adjusts the volume. She moves the relaxation mats to one side for the tea dancers. Dancing is a doing thing. I can hear her singing.

In Love

I T BEGAN IN a cinema.

She was working in the sweetie kiosk at the time, exchanging cash for Bassets and salting popcorn. A man walked up and asked for an extra large box, and because the machine was empty she had to tip some new, hard yellow corn into it and wait for it to heat up and explode. He missed the beginning of the film because of that. It was *Alien 2*. After the show he returned to the kiosk, where she was tipping the last of the coffee out of the jug into her mouth. He talked about the film for a bit, about how disgusting the alien was, like a cross between a slug and a vacuum cleaner. He said his name was Russell and asked if she'd like to go for a drink.

They had a lot in common and they would talk for hours. They both had one green eye and one blue eye. If they stood side by side the colour scheme was amazing.

This does not explain why she found him kissing her flatmate in the kitchen one afternoon, a few months later.

You know how it is. You lock yourself away in your room, but after a short time – three weeks or so – you have to go out to get some milk and find yourself fixing a big frightening smile on your face when you see them holding hands in the street.

In February her flatmate said, 'I can't stand the strain,' and moved out. Everything had ice on it, even eyelashes.

She began a new job that month at the delicatessen, cutting

cheese and salami instead of popping corn. The way life continued churned her up. Russell didn't even know she worked in the delicatessen; he didn't know the details any more, like the broken washing machine and the flat-cat having to wear a plastic collar round its neck. She couldn't tell him about the ham slicer or the deli owner, Mr Popolov, whose fingers looked like pale gherkins, delving amongst the olives and Baba Gnosh. The job was better paid than the one at the cinema, but you had to be clean and presentable; you had to wear see-through gloves to cut the cheese, and poke plastic name tags into the pâté. Mr Popolov was a man with a face like a side of ham, and kind. He told her about Russia, and gave her cuts of turkey breast.

After a while she started seeing her ex-flatmate's ex-boyfriend who was French. His name was Jean-Pierre. They had confusing gaps in their vocabulary so they just used to pull bits of wax off restaurant candles and try to reconstruct them again. When she told Jean-Pierre about her work at the deli, he didn't say anything about Russia or turkey breasts. He just talked about his work. They had nothing in common. She was tired but she couldn't sleep. Sometimes her face got screwed up so she couldn't see or swallow properly. This happened when she dropped rye bread on the floor, or when she ran for the bus and it went anyway and splashed her newly washed dress with puddle water.

At the end of one pale week she and Jean-Pierre went to a matinee of *The Snow Queen*. They sat watching people slide across the stage in large, terry-towelling goose costumes.

'They look very like bears, white bears,' said Jean-Pierre.

'Polar bears?' she said.

'Yes,' said Jean-Pierre. 'Polar bears.'

They sat gnawing walnut whirls, surrounded by children.

When she got home she found a message pinned to the kitchen board.

'Russell rang,' it said. 'Wants to know if you'd like to go to the cinema this evening. Phone back.'

So the four of them ended up sitting on more narrow mauve seats, this time at the Odeon. They all shared a large box of

101

popcorn and she felt as if she'd eaten too many because she had that bulge in her throat again, preventing her from swallowing. The film was French with bad sub-titles, and Jean-Pierre laughed when the rest of the cinema remained silent. A man in a stripy apron and a woman with neat cheekbones were having a conversation. The woman was thumping a large fish with a wooden spoon.

'Stop hitting that trout,' said the sub-titles.

'On the behind?'

'Everywhere, and with that handle!'

Jean-Pierre didn't laugh at that but Russell did, and he sidled some more popcorn out of the big box, and she felt his fingers scratching against the cardboard, against her legs. Kate and Jean-Pierre were muttering in the dark and the back of her seat moved when they laughed. She said, 'My boss has an apron like that one.' She wanted to talk, after the film, about the delicatessen and Mr Popolov's warty gherkin fingers. The cinema put her at ease; it was warm and dark and filled with crinkling sweet-wrapped sounds. 'Rustle, rustle,' she said – then she remembered that that was his name.

'Yes?' said Russell, 'What?' and they were sitting with their eyes in the blue green green blue sequence which used to make her feel that there was something significant, something mysterious about the two of them, but when he turned his head to look at her, she thought 'I don't love you any more.' She just thought it suddenly. That's how it goes. That's how it goes sometimes.

Optical Illusions

W E HAVE TO wear our names on the front of our waitressing gear. Mine says, 'Hello! My name is,' then there is a gap. The supervisor, Mrs Crawford, biroed my name in the wrong place, so it slips just below the edge of the card. Adults are told never to let their children wear T-shirts with their names on them, in case creeping old men lure them into their Morris Minors. The same should apply to waitresses, particularly since 75% of the 'clientele' here are creeping old men.

My name is Rachel. Everyone here calls me Rache, and it's usually strung on the end of a waitressing sentence, like,

'Table Two to go, Rache,'

or

'Can you check we've got enough dessert spoons in the basket, Rache?'

I'm sitting beside the Cona coffee machine, reading a book called *Fancy That!* It is full of optical illusions. There are pictures in it of creeping old men who also look like young girls, and rabbits that also look like squirrels. You can't see both images at once. The brain can't cope with all that information. But it helps to pass the time.

This is my tea break. I am allowed twenty minutes, somewhere between six hours' waitressing, because it's the law. The restaurant is a cross between an American Diner and Jo's Café. The spotty tables and plastic flowers are American, the bacon and eggs and greasy chips are British.

I've got to the end of my chapter, called 'Apparent Movement.' You're meant to stare at shapes with lines in them, like spirals and grids, and the shapes are supposed to move or suddenly develop different colours. It's mildly interesting, I suppose, but it doesn't seem to work with me. Or perhaps I've been here so long that things just look weird anyway.

'Does something appear to be running between the sets of lines?' the book queries, beneath a picture of six stripey rectangles. I think the answer must be 'Yes,' otherwise the question wouldn't be there in the first place. But I can't see anything. Perhaps the corner I am in is too dark.

It is comforting though, like a simple text book. I am holding the stripey rectangle page under the light of the coffee machine when Mrs Crawford sweeps magnificently past.

'I think you've had long enough now, Rache,' she says. 'Time to give Cathy a break.'

She swivels her enormous boobs and the rest of her follows. She bellows into the kitchen, 'Cathy, 20 minutes.'

Then she creaks away in her pink managerial dress.

Almost instantly, the kitchen door swings open and Cathy runs to the staff table, rummaging for a packet of cigarettes in her pocket. She is the cook, responsible for getting the orders out on time. Her face is flushed and her mascara has run. The smell of frying onions in the kitchen is overwhelming. I can hear Billy, the kitchen assistant, re-tuning the radio from the local station to Radio One.

'What are you reading, Rache?' Cathy asks, frantically puffing a Marlboro.

I tell her it's called *Fancy That!* The chapter I'm on is called 'Apparent Movement.'

'Sounds a bit like your waitressing.' She is a snide character. Sometimes I think I'd rather be alone with Mrs Crawford. At least Mrs Crawford is reliably tyrannical, lumbering violently through the small restaurant, clashing plates together, shrieking.

I put the book away to work on the cutlery basket. It is my job to make sure it is ready and glittering at all times. Each knife, fork and spoon set has to be wrapped up in a red paper napkin, and there is a separate section for long teaspoons, for eating ice cream and our speciality, eiderdown-thick milk shakes.

I am wrapping together some stray forks when a man taps me on the shoulder. 'This knife is dirty,' he says, clutching the offensive item. He is dirty too. His hands are grey and hairy and covered in oil. I am surprised by his high standards of knife cleanliness. But I don't say so.

I just say, 'Would you like to select another knife then?'

Perhaps this sounds impolite. I don't know. But I see Mrs Crawford out of the corner of my eye, slinking round a corner and taking note.

'Thank you . . . Rachel,' says the man, squinting ostentatiously at my left breast. Then he trundles back to his ketchup-covered egg and chips. He is too basic to appreciate the little pot of heather I put on his table earlier, when the restaurant had been virtually empty.

Outside, the shopping mall is playing Handel's Water Music through the loudspeaker system so everyone thinks they are rich and having a good time. It is switched off abruptly and replaced by 'I saw Mummy kissing Santa Claus.' The mall is open late for panicking Christmas shoppers, who are clicking quickly across the slippery floor into shop entrances. They don't look as if they are having a good time, buying things for God-knows how many twice-removed cousins and neighbours they don't want to offend. Little bottles of geranium moisturising cream which look more expensive than they are. Autumn Bouquet pot pourri mixtures. In shop windows there are signs saying EVERY-THING REDUCED. Tiny handbags and fairy shoes.

There are several people sitting round the phone kiosk. It is a low, moulded plastic contraption with four 'booths' at each corner. A Chinese girl, in a red raincoat, looks bored as she waits for one of the booths to empty. When I turn to face the restaurant again, I am aware of some sort of commotion going on at Cathy's table. She looks hot and angry, and she is talking aggressively to Mrs Crawford, who stands with her hands on her hips.

My vision has little glowing telephone booths in it. I've been staring at them too long, and now they impose themselves upon the two gesticulating women. They float downwards, from chair level to the floor, and when I blink, they start all over again. Little telephone ghosts. They hover for ages.

Cathy is embarrassingly loud. Some of the depressed eaters raise their heads from their food troughs and look for the noise. At the most remote table in the room, next to the Ladies and Gents, a middle-aged couple looks lost and lonely. They ignore Cathy's raised voice and continue with their grilled tomatoes, chewing slowly, their eyes fixed on invisible things. Scattered underneath the table are bags containing wrapping paper and cellophane boxes.

I collect a few plates from tables, pretending the scene in the corner does not exist. The plates are grim, bits of egg yolk and Daddy's Sauce smeared round the edges. I never get used to it. At one table, a woman drinking coffee asks me if I know what's going on.

'I think it must be the stress of Christmas,' I say, smiling like a martyr and sweeping a few raisins onto her lap with a damp cloth.

As I swing into the kitchen Mrs Crawford is hissing like a piece of bacon under the grill. She looks angrily around the restaurant with bulging eyes.

'Look, Cathy, I just didn't realise how many customers we'd get this evening. I'm asking you to do one extra hour. I'll pay you overtime.'

'Well that's just too bad,' says Cathy, 'because my boyfriend is coming to pick me up in five minutes and there's no way I'm staying just because you didn't plan ahead properly.'

The argument makes me feel cold and I dive into the kitchen, stacking the plates into the big silver dishwasher and shoving the rack through. When I go out into the restaurant again, Cathy is taking her apron off. She chucks it into the laundry basket by the coat rack, then pulls her jacket off a peg.

'That's it, then, Rache,' she says. 'I'm off.'

She is triumphant but her voice is shaking. She sweeps grandly out of the restaurant door, upright, with watery eyes. She doesn't say goodbye. This is the last I will see of her. Mrs Crawford is talking to herself, and swearing, polishing plant leaves in a frenzy at the till. She is almost frightening. When I walk past she grabs me and pushes me, as if I'm a vacuum cleaner, through the kitchen door. We are face to face by the frying pans.

'No doubt you heard that little episode, Rachel,' she says, folding her chins into the top of her apron. Her face is angular and dented as a cheese grater, behind a pair of pink-rimmed glasses. Sometimes, when she looms her jowls at me, I stop listening and just watch the strain in her eyes. Behind the pink, they are green and desperate.

'You'll have to help in the kitchen,' she's saying. 'Have you done much cooking for large numbers?'

So I find myself at the draining board, learning how to cook for large numbers, chopping up onions and peeling potatoes. Billy has been promoted to head cook. He stands at the huge, hot hob, shuffling an oily pan of eggs around.

'So Cathy got the sack then, eh?' he asks me, giving the vat of baked beans a quick stir with the egg spatula.

'Looks like it.'

I am wary of Billy. It is likely he will slap my bum if we stand together at the cooker. He is singing to a tune on the radio, and suddenly stops to say, 'I'm leaving as well.'

It seems Christmas is the time for escape.

'Don't leave me, Billy.' I'm genuinely pleading, fluttering my eyelashes and getting to grips with a large onion. 'Don't leave me to the mercy of Mrs Crawford.'

The radio on the shelf is covered in grease. Somehow a voice manages to emerge through it.

'Now, here's one of my favourites,' says the presenter, revelling in his jolliness. 'Frosty the Snowman.'

'What is this?' asks Billy and he snatches the dial onto another channel. He tunes into the end of 'So here it is, Merry Christmas, everybody's having fun . . .'

The onions are horrendously strong, the big, bright Spanish

107

kind which turn into little rivers when you cut them. I brush my eyes with the edge of my cuff but it just makes them sting even more.

'Strong, aren't they?' says Billy. 'It's much better if you cut them under running water.'

'I've heard you're meant to put a knife between your teeth.'

'Well that's just asking for trouble, isn't it?' And then he gives me a quick slap.

He's about four years younger than me, and about ten years more arrogant.

'I'm going to be sous-chef at the Argyll Hotel in January,' he tells me. 'I might be able to smuggle you some free dinners there if you play your cards right.' He hums back to the baked beans.

I turn on the tap. The water is freezing but it takes away the sting of the onions. I can see again.

Billy switches on the air extractor. It's as hot and smoky as Hell in here. There are no windows, just a circle in the swing door, which looks out into the restaurant. Through the circle, I can see Mrs Crawford, like a large goldfish collecting plates. Her thin chignon is falling out. Not one of the customers talks to her. The floor vibrates when she stomps across it. I see her advancing towards the door and leg it back to the onions.

'Table Four want two Christmas Bucks Fizz Sundaes,' she says, flatly, over her shoulder, then she launches herself through the door again. It makes a squashy noise as it flaps back into place.

'Can you do those?' asks Billy. He explains. Two scoops of vanilla ice cream, a splodge of chocolate sauce and some black cherry sauce. Then squirt cream over them.

'And they need some sparklers.'

He emerges from the store cupboard, waving some metal sticks at me.

'Are you sure?' I say. It's not Mrs Crawford's style.

'It's Christmas, isn't it? That's why they're called Christmas Buck's Fizz. Anyway, this is my last day here. I can do what I want.'

I walk flat-footedly across the broken floor to the freezer. Inside there are dozens of half-empty boxes of ice cream. They squeak painfully as I turn them over, looking for the vanilla. Eventually I find it, wedged between a Genuine Austrian Streudel and an Arctic Roll.

The chocolate and cherry sauces are waiting on the hob. I pour both over the ice cream and watch it all melt together. It looks like the little tubes you can buy at the beach, containing layers of coloured sand.

'Is that OK?' I ask Billy.

'Nice one,' he says, and he advances on them with a container of pressurised cream, squirting a large, white beehive on each. We stick six sparklers into the cream and light them with a Cook's Match. They spit at us innocently. Tiny little yellow sparks. 'Go on, then, before they go out.'

Billy shoves me through the door. I've still got my oniony apron on. I get a couple of ice cream spoons from the basket, ignoring wisecracks from the dirty knife man. Table Four is the lonely middle-aged couple by the toilets. I arrive at their side, feeling like a firework display.

'Sparklers!' says the woman.

Amazing what a bit of fire can do, even in this crummy place. A couple of fat business men have got paper hats from somewhere, about the same purple as their faces. And a group of girls, celebrating their last day at work, are screaming and shrieking with red Christmas tree baubles dangling from their ears. I go round the tables collecting empty plates and glasses with redundant straws in them.

When I push through to the kitchen again, a tray of eggy plates in my hands, Mrs Crawford is in there, reprimanding Billy for the sparklers. He is just standing there, with his hands behind his back.

'I am the one who decides when to put sparklers in the ice cream,' she is saying. Her pink dress has a blob of squirty cream on the front. A black hair-grip hangs by a fine, pale hair, and bangs against the side of her ear. Billy has propped my book up behind the spatulas, and it looks as if it is just about to slide forward and fall on her head. He's got it open at the chapter called 'Can You Believe Your Eyes?'

'I am the manager here.' She is huge and pink, like a big Christmas tree fairy. 'So no more smart ideas, OK, Billy, even if it is what they call the Festive Season.'

Something about her flopping hair, her sarcasm, makes me smile. Billy is silent. From behind his back, he produces another Christmas Bucks Fizz Sundae. It's kind of rudely extravagant, with five sparklers poked into the cream. He puts the glass down by the hob and lights the sparklers.

'For you,' he says.

Then he pulls my book out from behind the spatulas, and takes it with him back down to the deep fat fryer. Mrs Crawford and I stare at the yellow flecks for a minute. She has gone very quiet, as if she has been deflated like a bicycle tyre. She breathes peacefully through her nose. I turn away and there are little blue images, like fireflies, dancing behind my eyes. When I look back again, Mrs Crawford has unwrapped a dessert spoon from its red napkin and is licking a tiny piece of cream off the end of it. Her face looks different. There appears to be something running slowly behind her glasses.

'I'm sorry,' she's saying, 'I'm sorry.'

What Made You Come Here?

TODAY IS BEAUTIFUL, warm-smelling; there are pigeons in the trees with their claws wrapped around small branches. People are walking through the park, happy! and Jane feels that if she stares at them too long they might think there is something odd about her. She feels like someone shambling and peculiar. Her black eye doesn't go with anything, not anything nice, and sometimes she considers wearing a patch. She thinks that would make her less noticeable.

In the Eye Unit she is called in very quickly to see a nurse, who has a chart with a picture of two eyeballs. The nurse looks embarrassed about Jane's eye. She does not know what to say; this is not the right ward for asking whether someone has hit you. The nurse writes down Jane's name and address, then she scribbles a messy line around the right eyeball. Next, she holds up small, thick glasses that make Jane feel like a dictator, and says, 'Read the chart, please.' The letters are reflected in a mirror on the opposite wall, while the real letters are above her head; the reason for this is unclear – maybe it is part of the test. A, says Jane, then she reads the next few rows.

n? she says, m? o?

The nurse writes something down and tells Jane to go outside.

Whatever Jane looks at has a small purple hill in front of it. In the waiting room, the magazines are all purplish anyway, and

111

they flop a little underneath stains from spilled tea and too much fingering. They all have stories in them about men who are actually doctors but go on boating holidays and younger women called Morag who send letters to them. The younger women thought they were just friends but it turns out to be *Love Ahoy!*

People are sitting and sighing. Many have white lumps of cotton wool on their faces, and some are wearing dark glasses. A child slides about on his father's lap, eating Smarties and dropping several on the carpet. His father says, 'Try and open your good eye,' and the boy ignores him; he just crams Smarties in his mouth until there are none left, then he starts chewing the packet. It makes her want to cry. Apart from the boy and Jane and a man with a crash helmet, people are old. They sit mainly in couples, whispering to each other and eating biscuits from the canteen. One man sits by himself, staring with brown eyes into the nurse's room and beyond it, through all the corridors. He does not blink. His hands are still, on his knees. After quarter of an hour he stands up and walks slowly across the grey carpet and through the swing doors in the direction of Men's Toilets. As soon as the door has settled shut, a nurse walks into the waiting room and shouts, 'Mr Graham?'

There is no answer. Jane can see the man through the glass, in the distance, opening the door of Men's Toilets and walking in. The nurse ticks something on a sheet and disappears. The man's tea sits on the low table. Everyone stares at it as if it will maybe turn into Mr Graham and walk into the examining room. Everyone stares at the tea. After five minutes the man returns and sits down. Nobody speaks.

Jane thinks about eating a scone. There are fruit ones and plain ones, served by two women who have permed hair and perfect eyes. Nothing wrong with them at all. They seem to delight in being healthy, as if it might be contagious and will perhaps cure everyone if they sit there long enough. Perhaps you just need to touch something the women have touched. A KitKat bar. Jane goes to the hatch.

'Can I have a KitKat, please?' she says, and the woman says,

'You certainly can,' and pretends not to notice that Jane has a black eye. She passes Jane the KitKat on a paper plate and says it'll be 15p. A snip at the price.

There are other things to buy at the canteen. Brownies, fruit, sandwiches, hot soup. Jane creeps away with the chocloate bar and the women resume talking. They are discussing one of their daughters, who is going out with someone not very nice. Jane can't imagine why they want to work here. When she sits down she clears her throat and speaks to the man with the cup of tea.

'Are you Mr Graham?' she says, and she is aware of dark glasses and cotton wool pads turning, very slightly, in their direction.

She tells Mr Graham that the nurse was looking for him.

'Oh,' he says, and he looks at her black eye for a second. 'Oh,' he says. Then he gets up, gazing at a poster that says *Look After Your Eyes*, and walks into the nurse's room. Jane can hear the nurse's voice but not what she is saying. All she can see around the purple hill is Mr Graham's elbow. The nurse's voice stops, and she leads Mr Graham away down the corridors. She carries a clip board with both hands. Mr Graham's shoes sound like squid against the lino but the nurse knows about the floor's properties and wears hard soles.

People who arrived after Jane are going in before her. The little boy comes out of the examination room with his father. His eyes are still shut and he is chewing the head of a plastic monster. His father sees Jane staring and she looks down at her hands. She can feel her heart bumping, and there is a stale taste of chocolate in her mouth. She picks up another of the magazines and looks at a page entitled *Woman and Lifestyle*.

Everybody knows something about diet, after all, we need food and water to survive. We hear and read about what we should and shouldn't eat almost daily!

There is a page on Tips for a Pretty Salad. It tells you how to make Apple Wings, Leek Bows and Turned Mushrooms.

The man with the crash helmet is called in. He is holding

a piece of gauze against the side of his face and when he walks onto the lino his leather boots scream. A woman in a knee-length beige skirt presses buttons for the lift and when it arrives she steps in cautiously. Jane watches her creasing her eyes up behind her glasses, looking for numbers, then the doors shut and she disappears. God knows in which direction. Two more people arrive in the waiting room with eye patches.

When the nurse calls, Jane is not prepared. She has brought too many things with her: a jacket, a jumper, a shoulder bag, an overnight bag, a bag full of groceries. She can't sort it all out quickly enough. The magazine seems to attach itself to her fingers, gets knotted up with the handle of her bag and she can feel the nurse standing there in her blue uniform, fingering her watch, waiting, while she untwists, undithers, finally gets the magazine on the table with its falling-out inserts and knitting patterns. She gets to the door and the nurse is just an ankle around a corner, like the white rabbit.

In the examination room, Jane is introduced to a man wearing a white coat. His trousers look neat underneath, as if everything is all right in his life. He switches off the lights and tells Jane to sit down on a swivel chair in front of a black machine. 'Lean forward,' he says, 'and put your chin on the chin rest.' He squeezes orange drops in her eyes, then he shines lights into them, and the liquid heats up to the temperature of blood. A sea of different colours, tiny splashes of blue and pink wave at the blackness in her head. The consultant has turned her eyelids delicately around with cotton buds, as if they are a pair of roller blinds. He flips switches and lights shine at Jane from different angles and it is worrying, not being able to blink. She remembers someone telling her once that if you sneezed and didn't blink, your eyes would fall out.

The consultant stares at her irises through a microscope. It is almost romantic.

'What made you come here?' he says suddenly.

'What do you mean?' says Jane.

'Is it just the appearance that bothers you? People have a lot more to contend with,' says the consultant. 'You can see perfectly well, can't you?' he says. 'That's the main thing.'

He doesn't ask how her eye got like this; he doesn't say 'was it a door or someone close to you?' He doesn't want to know about causes for things. He unfurls her eyelids.

On her way out of the hospital, Jane walks into the men's toilets. There is a sign outside of a person wearing trousers, and something flips, something in her head says, 'I am wearing trousers: I am allowed in here.' She can see perfectly well; it is just her mind misinterpreting things. Mr Graham is in there again, washing his hands vigorously with coal tar soap. 'Oh,' he says, when he sees Jane.

'Hallo,' says Jane. She steps forward and peers at her eye in the mirror. It doesn't look any different, but she feels something changing. She blinks a few times. There are still splashes of colour inside her head, but the colours are like a kaleidoscope now, changing all the time.

'Bye, love,' says Mr Graham, walking past her to the door. 'Don't let them get you down,' he says.

'Right,' says Jane, because she can think of nothing else. Strangers seem to have a habit of saying things like that, mildly philosophical things that you might remember years later, or that you might always connect with something curious, like a tiled hospital wall or a certain time of year. This particular afternoon, Jane just stands there by the mirror, watching Mr Graham get smaller and smaller as he walks down the corridor. She is thinking about where she will go from here.

Very Flyaway

T HE SALON WAS always being decorated for celebrations. On St Valentine's Day, Maureen hung hearts over the mirrors. They were made out of some shiny paper that looked solid, like a sheet of metal, but the heat of the hairdryers made them flop after a while. The hearts were supposed to lure people in for romantic haircuts, but that morning there was just a perm and a woman wanting her long hair cut short. In the end she had a half-inch trim. 'That's much better,' she said, uncertainly, to her reflection. Little snips of dark hair floated in her coffee.

Maureen's shoes clicked all morning. She wore Blakies on the heels of her shoes and made dents in the lino. She went to dance classes, and during coffee breaks she showed the hairdressers the steps she knew – Paddy Barr and Front Cross Step. She hopped from one foot to the other and the Blakies sounded like drawing pins on the tiles.

'Have you got a nail or something stuck to your shoe?' Michelle asked, wrapping a towel roughly round someone's head and guiding them to a mirror.

'No,' said Maureen, 'they're Blakies.'

'That's what kids put on their shoes, isn't it?' said Michelle. 'To make sparks.'

Maureen did not reply. She lifted her feet out of the way of a long-handled broom that was being pushed around the floor. The hair always built up like snow against a snowplough, and she didn't want to be caught up in it.

*　　*　　*

The salon was called The Cut Above but Maureen called it 'the saloon' because it looked like something out of the Wild West, like a scene where John Wayne burst through the swing doors with two revolvers. There were melon-shaped sections cut out of the walls, and slatted wood; it seemed like the kind of place where you would order Tequila with limes. Michelle said that chrome and black were out. 'So eighties,' she said, swerving on her castored chair from one wet head to another. 'Outdated.' Now it had distressed walls and basins with a rustic design.

'Is this what the nineties look like?' Maureen said. She looked around the room: people were peering at themselves with frightened expressions.

'This is the caring nineties, Maureen,' said Michelle in a mock voice, pretending to be someone else. She was the top stylist, whose hair reached all the way down her back and hung, heavy and uncut. She wore tight tops underneath transparent plastic, and Maureen had seen women's eyes following her in the mirrors. She smelled of soap and looked disconnected, somehow, from the scrunched-up, overheated aspects of life. She was blank and pale and her sentences would find their way to Maureen's heart and stab like skewers.

Maureen had developed a way of not looking at herself in the mirrors, of just staring at heads and washing. The salon got crowded at the end of the week, and all six basins were occupied with heads, vulnerable and disconnected by beige ceramic. The hairwashers got commission for every bottle of shampoo and conditioner they sold so they had to find something to say about hair; they had to criticise it gently. There was a fine balance between advice and rudeness, but Maureen, after four years at The Cut Above, had got good at it. Sally, who also swept hair off the floor, was still learning.

'Your hair is very greasy,' Sally said to a woman one evening. The woman already had a red face and was looking desperately up at the light fittings. 'It's greasy on top,' Sally continued, 'but very dry and split at the ends.'

'I know,' said the woman, and she shut her eyes, as if the salon might have gone away when she opened them again.

117

'Can I ask what kind of hair product you are using?' said Sally.

'No,' said the woman. Her features seemed to be stretched tightly across her face. Her skin was smooth and shone like a pink moon. Sally stopped talking and rinsed the woman's hair with water that was slightly too hot, then tied a large towel around her head. The woman was obedient now, like a child. She was led down to the basement where she had her hair scraped back and a large rubber sheet placed across her shoulders.

'Michelle will be with you in a minute,' Sally said, and did not offer her a coffee or a magazine.

Maureen sometimes dreamed of becoming a professional dancer. At classes on Tuesday nights, the tutor said she had natural rhythm; she picked up new steps easily while other people were still leaping into the air at the wrong moment, or confusing back steps with front ones. They all stood in a large circle and stared at the tutor's feet, then tried to imitate her. Sometimes the tutor brought a fiddle into class, and would play a tune and dance at the same time. Her fingers and feet tapped out exactly the same rhythm and Maureen admired the way her flat, flat shoes managed to make a clicking sound; that was when she bought the Blakies. After class she would drive home, a little pink and breathless, and she would show her husband the steps while he was watching television. Their flat was carpeted though, and it wasn't the same. In the community hall everyone stomped on the wooden floor as if they wanted to break through to the other side of the world.

'The good thing about this kind of dancing,' said the tutor, 'is that you don't have to be young to pick it up.'

'That's a relief,' said Maureen to the woman standing next to her.

The woman smiled quickly and said 'Ha.' They all attended the classes regularly, but no-one really talked, apart from a group of women who already knew each other. The others ran away at the end of the evening, like frightened mice, into the darkness. Maureen asked the tutor if it was easy to make a living from this kind of dancing, and the tutor looked apprehensive.

'What do you do at the moment?' she said.

'I work in a hairdressers,' said Maureen.

'I've always thought it must be really satisfying, cutting hair,' said the tutor, then she somehow drifted away; she just moved across the hall, to the group of women who knew each other. They weren't taking it seriously. They had linked their arms together and were kicking their legs out like a chorus line. They were all wearing bouclé jumpers.

At midday most of the hairdressers ate sandwiches in the staff-room, surrounded by the smell of chemicals and hot hair. Maureen couldn't stand it. At lunchtime she always went outside, to breathe in the thin, grey air of the city. Sometimes she booked a table at Luigi's. You could see it from the salon window. It had a cheap lunch menu and served good pizza. There was also a green parrot called Eccolinni, that sat in a cage and imitated the squeak of the front door. The staff liked to place customers at the table next to Eccolinni, particularly those that looked as if they might have come for a romantic meal. On St Valentine's Day, Eccolinni's table had the quickest turn-around.

'I don't think that bird is very hygienic,' a woman said to the waitress one lunchtime. She was sitting at the table next to Maureen's in a black embroidered dress, twirling tagliatelle hopelessly onto her fork. 'Isn't there some skin rash,' she said to the waitress, 'some kind of disease you can get from parrots?'

'I think they're quite clean birds actually, said the waitress, and she sighed. She had not worked in the restaurant for long; she was still not sure where they kept the spare pepper pots, where they put the parmesan at the end of the day. She turned, tugging her skirt with her hands to make it longer, and flipped through the swing door. Luigi was in the kitchen, talking in Italian with the chef. From her table, Maureen could hear the word 'Goal.' Perhaps there was no word in Italian for goal.

'Hey, Maureen' Luigi said, coming out of the kitchen with a flat dish of minestrone. 'You are beautiful today.'

Maureen looked up from her menu and said 'Sorry?' She never knew how to deal with compliments. There was some reflex action, some twitching disbelief in what people said about her. Her hair needed re-styling. She had lines on her face. Her knees were pointed as tooth picks, and her calf muscles did not show the way they should, not curvy and strong. She smiled briefly then looked at the anchovies on her pizza. Beyond the tables she could see the chef in the kitchen, moulding dough with his hands. There was an oven on the back wall that looked like a white cave or an igloo. The chef threw lumps of dough into it and they come out as bread, or he slid pizza bases in there. It intrigued her. If she turned her head slightly to the left, she would see people working in the Cut Above, but she always averted her eyes.

'Table eight needs a mixed salad,' the waitress said, through a hatch, and Luigi turned around.

'Eccolinni's table,' he yelled. He delivered the minestrone, then rubbed his hands and swung away. His trousers were too tight and he wore a silk shirt. When he came out of the kitchen again, Maureen ordered pudding – pear soaked in crème de menthe.

'Are you doing something nice for Valentine's Day?' Luigi asked.

'I'm going to my dance class,' Maureen said, 'then maybe my husband and I will do something later.'

'Your husband and you will do something later,' Luigi repeated. 'Well,' and Maureen felt herself blushing like a teenager. She had never grown out of sounding naïve; she was always setting people up for clever retorts.

'Well,' said Luigi, 'have a nice time.'

In the corner of the room, Eccolinni squawked, like the wicked witch of the east. Luigi brought Maureen the pear soaked in crème de menthe and said it was 'on the house.'

'I didn't know you could dance,' he said. 'Maybe you should put on a show for us one day.'

He did not take her seriously. The pear was the same colour as his shirt; Maureen sliced it with her spoon, and one half slid upwards in the glass, like a fish.

*   *   *

She was late. When she got back to the salon, there were three women sitting in beige smocks waiting for their hair to be washed. They looked like characters from a very long opera.

'Maureen,' Michelle said, emerging from the staff-room in her transparent overall, 'these ladies are all waiting.'

Her eyes were round and fringed with mascara. Clipped onto her top pocket were some metal implements and there were also some hair rollers in there, underneath the plastic. The three women's eyes rolled timidly towards Maureen, then back to Michelle, where they remained.

'Right,' said Maureen, 'who's first?'

'Maureen,' said Michelle, and she glared at her, with something that looked like hatred. 'Be polite,' said her eyes.

'Right,' said Maureen to the woman nearest her, 'this way please.'

The woman swiftly gathered all her possessions up – her handbag, her shopping and her coat, and followed Maureen to the basin. When she leaned her head back, Maureen looked at the woman's hair. It was very fine, with a few flecks of grey in it. She could have recommended Body-Building Shampoo for Flyaway Hair but she didn't have the energy. The woman didn't look as if she would buy anything from her anyway. From this position all she could see of her face were the sharp angles: the triangle of her forehead, the slant of her eyebrows and the tip of her nose and chin. If the women raised her eyes, she would just see the soft underside of Maureen's chin, her nostrils, the creases under her eyes. It was strange talking to someone whose head was upside-down.

But the woman spoke anyway.

'You don't like working here, do you?' she said.

'Would you?' said Maureen.

'If I liked washing people's hair I would,' said the woman.

Maureen thought she was perhaps pummelling the woman's head a little roughly, as if she was making bread.

'Oh well,' she said, and she checked the temperature of the water against her wrist. It was too hot, so she turned it down. 'Not many people end up doing what they want, do they?'

'No,' said the woman, and she stared up at the cracks in the ceiling.

'What do you do?' said Maureen.

'I am a violinist,' said the woman.

'See,' said Maureen. 'There's no comparison, is there?'

'What do you mean?' said the woman, and her eyebrows converged, creating tiny crevices across her forehead.

'You must enjoy it,' said Maureen.

'I suppose so.'

'I would,' said Maureen. 'Do you play reels?'

'I normally play in an orchestra,' said the woman.

'Do you know Staten Island?'

'No,' said the woman.

'That's what I am learning to dance to at the moment. Staten Island.'

'I see.'

Underneath the basin, inside her shoes, Maureen's toes squashed out a rhythm.

'See, if you're really interested in something,' she said, 'I'm sure you can turn it into a career.'

'Maybe,' said the woman. 'It depends.'

'That's what I'm planning to do anyway,' said Maureen, but the woman didn't reply. In the mirror, Maureen could see her closing her mouth.

After that they just spoke in short sentences. Maureen asked the woman to sit up, to hold her head forward. She told her she had very fine hair – 'Very flyaway,' she said, and she folded it up into a beige towel.

Flying Down the Flights

M Y FATHER USED to say I drank apple juice like water. Now someone's saying I drink wine like apple juice. I stop biting the edge of my polystyrene cup to see what the person looks like. He is a tall man with a beard, who is swaying by the mulled wine pan, or perhaps I am the one swaying. It's difficult to tell. He looks like King Lear, that's what I tell him, then I wander off to the bottle table to top up my red wine.

This particular track on the record seems to have been playing for the past hour, but I know that can't be right. Tracks usually only last a couple of minutes. I fill my cup up again, proud with myself for finding a nearly full bottle of drinkable stuff. Then I lean against the table, this time digging my fingernails into the polystyrene. I stand and watch people dancing.

Time slows down and speeds up without warning.

I have been standing in the same part of the room, staring at people dancing and an orange balloon attached to the wall, for hours. When I go into the bathroom, I focus with great clarity on all the bottles round the edge of the bath. Aapri Facial Scrub. Timotei Honey Hair Conditioner for Extra Bounce. V05 Apple Shampoo for Greasy Hair. You would think my life depended on memorising hair types.

It's good being alone in the bathroom. Civilised. Against the frosted glass of the door, I can see vague shadows of people in the queue, and I know that if they look through the glass, they will see an unstructured red stripy heap at the end of the thin

123

room, which is me. I take my time, gazing at the pretty plants in macramé pot holders on the back of the door, the yellow, bespectacled hippopotamus which, presumably, the owner of the flat plays with at bath time. There is a redundant, bakelite telephone beside me. I finger the thin, black telephone cord and pick the receiver up. Yes, it is dumb.

There is a knock on the door and a muffled voice says, 'Come on, there's a queue out here.'

I get up very quickly, rearrange my jeans and check my face in the cabinet mirror. Surprisingly, my eyes are not bloodshot, but I have a little pink rash around my collar bones, which was not there before. Stress rash. I pull my T-shirt higher over it and click the bolt back, then make a neat path though the crowds, like some biblical character parting the waves.

Biblical characters, of course, don't get stood up.

There are lots of girls sitting on the floor in the hall, chatting and laughing. I don't wish to join them. I am totally alone. I don't know this big white flat or the people in it. They all look peculiar, with tie-dye T-shirts and long hair that needs the V05 treatment. But I am determined to stay, to make myself feel even worse. If you are going to get stood up, it might as well be cataclysmic.

Back in the kitchen, King Lear takes my polystyrene cup from me and drags me into the middle of the room, swaying my arms about joyously, as if I am a consenting rag doll. A little group of expert dancers jump and slink around us, and I pretend that I am laughing. King Lear's beard has a tiny piece of orange peel in it, from the mulled wine. He tells me he is a zoologist, and I say it suits him, then twist my fingers out of his grasp and scuttle to the edge of the room.

In moments of peace, when a record has finished, I think of Jim. I shall never speak to him again. I am particularly annoyed with myself that I bought him such a stylish green shirt for his birthday, which he now wears all the time.

At the bottle table, a girl is pouring herself some Irn Bru into a Smarties mug. She says hallo, her name is Sue, and asks me if I am a VSO person.

I am confused, thinking of shampoo.

'A what?'

'A voluntary service person. Most people here seem to be, for some reason.'

'Oh, no, I'm not. I'm . . . I am . . . I do a bit of lots of things but I'm mainly unemployed.'

Sue finds me boring or strange for some reason, and turns away to roll herself a thin cigarette.

Drifting out of the kitchen again now, to look for the all but empty room. There is always an all but empty room. Parties always consist of: a crowded kitchen, a coupling cupboard, a row of outstretched legs in the hall and a dark room with murmuring conversations and maybe a cat.

And, oh God, King Lear is in there as well.

I sit on the window seat and find a cat, nearly hidden beneath some big green cushions which smell of smoke and heads. The cat and I stare through the window for a bit, almost finding something philosophical to think about the darkness which is almost dawn, and the stars. Then the cat jumps off my lap and King Lear advances with a saucer of salted almonds.

'Something to soak up all that wine,' he says. He is a kind man. He tells me his name several times, but I forget. Then he tells me about zoology and I forget that too. I say something about earthworms, and about a wormery I had once. You encourage them to come up by sprinkling water over the soil.

We eat salted almonds for a while, or maybe for a long time. There is a smell of satsumas and stewed wine, and in the kitchen someone has put on some very loud Motown music. A girl is pouring Saxa salt over a large wine stain on the carpet, and the salt turns grey, like slush on the pavements.

'Billy has a really rare juke-box,' says King Lear after a bit. 'It cost him nearly 500 quid.'

We go to look at the juke-box in Billy's bedroom. It reminds me of a cheese counter: the glass across the record stack is rounded, just like the ones in William Low's.

'Let's put a record on,' I say, and choose 'Sitting on the Dock of the Bay.'

After the button has been pressed, a thin metal arm swings the 78 into position on the turntable. Then the needle goes down and Otis Redding starts with his sad song.

I try to shut the glass lid but something is stopping it from shutting. It resists like an umbrella that won't go back the right way when the wind has blown it inside out. I feel, though, that if I can just shut the lid everything will be all right. So I keep pushing it. It refuses to click into place. It's beginning to annoy me, just when I'm supposed to be listening to the song, feeling soulful. Things always need so much more encouragement in other people's houses. Mulled wine needs more heat, the volume dial needs to be turned up higher, lids need to be shut with a firm hand.

Somewhere King Lear is saying, 'The records have to go back first,' and then the glass snaps. It snaps right the way across the centre. King Lear looks at me as if the scales have fallen from his eyes, and he doesn't follow me out of the room this time. There is the sound of tinkling glass behind me.

In the hall I am putting on my coat when the doorbell makes a little ringing sound and Jim walks in, wearing the green shirt I gave him. I have become so used to him not being here that now he seems out of place. And he has got in the way of standing me up, of abandoning me. He looks as if he is saying sorry, explaining something or other, but I can't hear him beneath the noise and he irritates me. It's too late. I'm too tired. I don't speak to him. There is something inside me that is beyond being hurt now, that makes me take off, fly past him. Just as I get to the door, I see King Lear creeping out of Billy's bedroom with the rest of the salted almonds and a dustpan and brush. Jim is staring at the dustpan and brush as if they might explode. Around them both are pink outraged faces, and a rumour being whispered through the air that someone has broken Billy's juke-box.

Strangely, my legs speed up without warning. I'm racing like a comet down all the flights of stairs, skipping and hopping across the sparkling granite staircase and when I get to the bottom I swing through the front door and down the steps as if I'm really flying. It must have been all that red wine I knocked back like fruit juice. I'm flying down the flights.

Battenburg Cake

H E'S ASLEEP WITH his mouth open, and a magazine about interiors. The girl looks at his face. A stiff paintbrush moustache, not the kind that ruffles in the wind. The eyelids are thin. When he opens them, his eyes are transparent like clear bottles. Once she had thought all grandfathers were like that, with that band of hair round their heads, with that low-high voice that bounces out of rooms.

She touches his arm and the magazine slides off his lap. She picks it up and puts it on a chair. Her grandfather takes a plastic tube out of his pocket, puts it in his mouth, presses it, breathes in, the tube hisses. He does it again. Then he puts the tube away. He never talks about this.

'Been sent in to find me?'

'U-huh.'

An ice-cream van is making sounds like cracked plates on the pavement. Ice cream, in ice-cream-coloured weather. The sky is full of gulls.

'They're a long way inland,' says her grandfather. 'Must be rough at sea.'

She imagines the Atlantic, black and rough and stuffed with grappling octopus and skate, while she is in this still room again with her grandparents' white-limbed ornaments and a skeleton clock. Everything moves in it: bits of brass and cogwheels and glass tubes.

'I'm bored,' she says.

'Helped your mum with the tea?'

'She was spilling milk.'

'I see.'

He moves his thin mouth as if he is about to make a speech. His hands clutch the roundness of the armchair.

'Shall we play scrabble?'

They keep board games behind the photograph cupboard. She drags a footstool to his armchair and drags another across the blotchy carpet so they face each other. The board creaks when she opens it, not like the one at home with tea stains and layers of paper ripped off.

'Seven, isn't it?'

He shunts letters around and lets her start. ZEBRA.

'Using your Z in the first move,' he says, clearing his throat and hovering his fingers above the board. He is serious.

After a minute, he says, 'Can I have ALZEBRA? Maths for zebras?'

'Grandpa!' She is too old for his jokes.

'All right,' he says. He clicks five letters across the squares. FLOWER.

The clock makes a grinding sound and she thinks it is about to chime but when she looks it is still only five to four; she always forgets that sound, five minutes before the hour.

He clears his throat. 'One of us better keep score,' he says.

He finds a piece of card and a felt pen in the box, and draws a line. The last game was headed HIM and HER. This time he writes initials.

She's got a depressing line of vowels in her tray, and groups them together. AAAIIEE. Like one of Tarzan's lines. What's yellow and swings from tree to tree? Tarzipan.

'Swop you a couple of consonants for a couple of vowels.'

'OK.'

The floor squeaks and her mother walks in with a floor cloth. Followed by her grandmother, slowly, giggling, behind a Battenburg cake. They eat Battenburg cake every time they visit. She likes to dissect the pink and yellow squares.

Grandmother puts the cake on a thin-legged table and cuts

129

six laborious slices. The marzipan bulges out like a pillow while her mother smiles and hangs on to the floor cloth.

'Your go,' says the grandfather and the girl picks out a C and a K and suddenly she's standing over the board, assembling C A K E across a double word score.

'Look,' she says. The grandfather whistles, breathes in, waves his fingers above the letter tray, pushes two squares on either side of the 'e.'

'Tea and Cake,' he says, and his thin mouth moves as if he is about to make a speech.

Therapeutic

I SIT WITH my head almost leaning against the window, but the glass is smeared and I don't let myself touch it, not even the tips of my hair. I want to get out of this train. I want someone to kiss me and carry my luggage. A beige plastic cup is rolling towards me. It leaks bits of coffee when the train swings outwards.

On the other side of the table a man is doing a tapestry. He has been doing this tapestry for two hundred miles. Since Doncaster. It is in a big wooden frame, which I imagine he hammered and sawed into shape like a thin Father Christmas making a sleigh. Maybe he has a wife who comes in with Ovaltine. Maybe he has a cat. The tapestry is sparkling: gold, yellow, bronze, and he is stitching small squares. He is wearing a checked shirt and crepe-soled shoes.

Outside a man walks along the river bank in a flat cap. He always seems to be there when I look out of train windows; I feel as if I should wave. The sky is white and cold. October. I look back into the compartment. Red and grey lines intersecting; a chain in a box, penalty for misuse £50. The automatic door has gone wrong and opens all the time. People walk past: crimplene backsides occasionally followed by children's heads. There is a smell of cheese from the buffet. The tapestry man sighs, puts his hands inside a plastic bag and chooses some more thread. Silver.

'So,' he says, and I jump.

'So,' he says, 'what are you studying?'

'Well,' I say, 'I'm not studying. I used to study, but I don't study any more.'

'Yes,' says the man, 'you look like someone who would study something.'

'Do I?' I say, then I laugh, high and false, and stare quickly out of the window. The man sucks the end of the silver thread, picks up his needle, and the thread bends for a few seconds before going through. For a while the train is quiet: I can just make out a Roxy Music song playing through someone's Walkman. The train slows down as it goes through a small station, but not slow enough for me to see the name on the platform. I know the man is going to say something else any minute. I am waiting for another comment. I don't like talking on trains: I like being silent, but this man wants to talk. He draws breath; I get ready to make a response but he doesn't say anything.

Then he draws another breath and says, 'Very therapeutic, embroidery.'

'Yes,' I say.

'Do you sew at all?'

'A bit of darning sometimes. I used to embroider when I was younger.'

'But you are not old now,' says the man.

'No,' I say, 'not that old.'

'A spring chicken,' says the man, 'a mere slip of a girl.'

'Mmm,' I say, and I try to adhere my gaze closer to the view, as if I am suddenly interested in a factory outside called the Universal Grinding Wheel Company Ltd. My hair touches the glass. It is cold outside. When I pull my hair round my shoulder, it leaves wispy imprints in the condensation.

'Travelling far?' says the man.

'Up to Edinburgh,' I say.

'I am getting off at the next stop,' says the man. 'I shall have to start packing up my bits and pieces in a minute.'

'I expect that takes a while,' I say. I want to be friendly now – now I know that we will not be travelling the next 150 miles together.

132

'I am going in for a competition,' says the man. 'We have to design a church hassock.'

He turns the frame round and holds it up for me to look at. There is a big square of empty canvas in the centre, and a few rectangles around it.

'I have a long way to go,' says the man. 'It is meant to say *Consider the lilies of the field, how they grow, they toil not, neither do they spin,* but I have to send it off by next Tuesday so I think I'm going to have to shorten it.'

'Right,' I say. 'Maybe just *Consider the lilies of the field* will be enough,' I say, 'because I think most people know it anyway, you know, the general gist.'

'Ah,' says the man, 'but is *the general gist* good enough for a church hassock?'

I can't think what to say. There is something strange about this man, as if he wants other people to hear him. He turns the frame round again and starts to pull thread through the canvas. It makes a pulling noise. I like the sound – it is precise, like a cat purring.

I have with me a laundry bag full of apples. They are bulging in this big flowery bag. On trains there is nowhere to put things like this. To prevent seven pounds of fruit from rolling around the carriage, I have had to tuck the bag behind my legs. I get one of the apples out of the bag, examine it for bird-pecks, then bite into it. It is cold against my teeth, and almost white inside. The apple is a little misshapen, slightly off-centre, but it tastes good.

'An apple a day,' says the man, snapping thread between his teeth, 'an apple a day keeps the doctor away. I wonder how old that saying is?'

'Mm,' I say. There is a tiny fleck of apple between my two front teeth.

'These old sayings often make a lot of sense,' says the man.

The train starts to slow down. A man with a stammer says, *Newcastle. Newcastle will be the next station stop.* The tapestry man starts to put away his threads. He wraps them round his

133

fingers and makes short skeins, then he puts them one by one into his plastic bag: gold, silver, yellow.

'Nearly there now,' he says. 'Nearly home.'

'It looks as if it's raining out there,' I say, trying to peer through the smears on the window. It is getting dark.

On the seat behind me there is a little girl talking to her mother. 'Look at the lights,' she says. 'They look like birds, golden birds flying.'

'I think you are hallucinating,' says her mother.

The man says, 'I hope the rest of your journey goes well.' He is still talking in a loud voice, as if he is on a stage. He turns his head to look at the other passengers. When he moves the tapestry frame, I see he has nearly finished the C of Consider. There is also something that looks as if it might be a lily in the top left-hand corner. The man smiles and says, 'I have my work cut out for me.'

'I've got about seven pounds of apples here,' I say suddenly. I don't know what makes me say this. 'Would you like one?' I say.

'No. No I won't, no thank you,' he says. 'They give me indigestion. I *need* a doctor if I eat apples.'

He laughs loudly. He picks up his tapestry frame. 'Goodbye,' he says. 'So nice to have met you.' He waits for the shuffle of people to go past then proceeds through the automatic door, which is now permanently wedged.

I watch him walking down the platform, with his frame and his bag of threads. The little girl behind me is singing, 'Bye bye Newcastle.' Then it's just me and this bag of apples. For some stupid reason, I feel lonely.

A Gap In Her Life

ROSE IS A proof-reader and her days are filled with strange facts. 'Oh,' she says to the man who shares her desk, 'did you know there is a place in South-East Asia called Bum Bum?'

'What?' says the man, after a while. He is old with rampant eyebrows.

'Doesn't matter,' says Rose, and she wonders what has happened to her sense of humour. At the moment she is working on something called *The Essential Home Reference Book*. Essential! It lists the administrative districts in Albania, and has an A to Z of phobias. Ergasiophobia: fear of work. Peniaphobia: fear of words. She has already found several for herself.

Rose has a friend called Ellen who is scared of nothing. Ellen is a normal person, so normal she even reassures herself. She stands by people, and she has stood by Rose, like a fence post, for the past two years. She has gone to Rose's house and listened to her with her head on one side, and hugged her and said, 'If there's anything I can do . . .' and Rose just wants her to go away. But Ellen enjoys challenges; she enjoys thankless tasks, and Rose is one of them. 'So,' she says seriously, like a doctor, 'how are you feeling now?' Sometimes she invites Rose to her house, where they sit clutching cups of tea and Ellen asks how she is. 'How are you coping?' she says, in a low voice, the kind you use when you are walking around a cathedral. Ellen's house is large and clean with glass vases full of catkin branches. Ellen

135

has parties sometimes, small, tinkling parties with a selection of salads. You have to wear a pretty dress if you are female, and something masculine and hand-knitted if you are male. 'Well,' says Ellen, 'I'm having a party on Friday,' and Rose knows that there will be a single man stashed away somewhere. It is two years now since her husband died, and this is long enough for Ellen. 'You should join an evening class,' says Ellen, 'or how about aerobics?' Maybe she thinks if you upholster enough chairs or bounce around for long enough on an exercise mat, you can forget about someone. Ellen does not mention any single man, but Rose knows there will be one at her house on Friday, sitting behind a fruit bowl. He will be called something sweaty and pale; Alec or Neil.

High House. Ellen's house is at the top of a flight of steps so it is called High House. There is a little pot of orange marigolds on each step, and when she gets there Rose just wants to sit outside with them all evening, with the marigolds and a bottle of wine. She rings the bell and waits. No-one appears. Inside, Ellen will be doing something important with avocados. It is half past nine in the evening but the sun is still shining. The sun always shines when she goes to Ellen's house; everything is always perfect. She stands and listens to the silence and wants to run away, down the steps. There is a cat on the pavement, washing its paws and she watches it for a while. Cats are so calm and so wise. After a couple of minutes she sees Ellen through the glass panels of the door. She is plodding towards her and holding an avocado. Rose doesn't know whether to smile, whether the glass between them is meant to transmit smiles. Ellen is not smiling. She turns the handle and opens the door and then she smiles.

'Rose!' she says. 'Halloooo.' She is holding an avocado.

'Hallo,' says Rose. Ellen kisses her on both cheeks, and her mouth says, 'Mwah, mwah,' and she pushes her into the hall. She continues pushing her all the way through the house until they reach the kitchen. 'Orange juice? Wine? Sherry?' says Ellen. She does not often use whole phrases.

In the kitchen there is a man sitting at the table, clutching a

136

place-mat. He is Ellen's husband. 'Hallo, Rose,' he says. 'How are you?'

'Fine, thanks,' she says. She can't remember what his name is. 'How are you?'

'Fine, thanks,' he says. They stop talking. They have established nothing.

Ellen hands Rose an orange juice, presented in the most tasteful way. It is in a large, rustic glass, with two slices of orange and an ice cube and a sprig of mint. It clinks, soothingly. There was a time when Rose drank too much, so Ellen gives her soft drinks when she can.

'Pistachio nuts?' she says, and she goes away, into another room.

'So,' says Ellen's husband. He swivels the place-mat between his index fingers. Rose suddenly remembers that his name is George. She wants to say a sentence with 'George' in it, just to show how on the ball she is.

'Pistachio nuts,' says Ellen, returning to the kitchen with a small patterned bowl.

The doorbell rings seven times in the space of ten minutes, and Rose wonders when Ellen's guests are going to stop appearing. They are like a crowd on an escalator when someone hits the emergency button. They crush their way, laughing, into the kitchen and spill out into the hall. They are introduced to each other, and smile cautiously and no-one retains names in their heads. They pour themselves drinks and stick vegetables into green and pink dips. There are seven men in hand-knitted jumpers and six women in pretty dresses. Rose can not work out which man is meant for her, but she thinks he may be the one, the only one, whose jumper has a slightly awkward pattern on it. He is standing pale and silent by the dips. Ellen's husband arranges seats in the living room and every so often checks on his goldfish. 'Still alive are they, George?' says one of the jumpered men, and he laughs. George doesn't say much; Rose notices that.

'I do love your dress,' a woman says to her, 'How pretty.'

'Thank you,' says Rose. She doesn't know what to say about

the woman's dress. It has pearl buttons which match her ear-rings.

'Isn't this nice?' the woman sighs, and as soon as she says this there is a sudden silence in the room. The man nearest Rose chops the end off his laugh and swills the ice cube fast around his glass. A woman standing underneath the clock says 'So' and focuses her eyes at some hazy point in the middle of the crowd. A lorry draws up outside the kitchen window and the driver does not switch the engine off. He just sits in his cab, parallel with the party guests, and shouts at someone they can't see. The lorry has *Forsyth's Fresh Fruit* written on the side, each word sharing the same enormous F. People smile and clear their throats. They stare at the lorry and clutch the stems of their wine glasses. The silence wavers for a moment and Rose is aware of Ellen hovering behind her, gripping the bowl of pistachio nuts and sensing danger. Ellen dreads lulls in conversations. Her parties must always be full of voices. She is just about to rush in with the pistachio nuts or a comment about gardening, when a man speaks in a slow, slow voice. 'Orsyth's Resh Ruit,' he says. 'Look,' he says, 'Orsyth's Resh Ruit.' He spells the words out in the air. When he lowers his arm, people laugh uncertainly and begin to talk again; they are all inspired at the same moment. Ellen puts the bowl down and frowns at the lorry driver through the window.

Rose fills a gap in Ellen's life. She is a mysterious window. She is also a young widow with dark hair, like Jackie Onassis, and that is even better. And if she seems slightly unhinged on occasion, that is an interesting thing to discuss with friends. Rose drinks tea with Ellen and tells her nothing. She knows Ellen would love to hear stories of her wandering around at four in the morning, or listening to the same record every day for a month.

'Rose,' says Ellen once she is sure the party conversation can support itself. 'This is Alec,' she says, and she trundles the man in the awkward jumper towards her. 'Alec is a conservatory consultant, Rose.'

'Oh,' says Rose.

'Rose is a proof-reader,' Ellen says to Alec, then she is suddenly not there any more, she is on the other side of the room, pleased with the introduction, neat in her buttoned blouse.

'So,' Rose says after a few seconds' silence. She doesn't know if she can sustain a polite discussion, not even for a minute. It is difficult to remain focused, not to become hypnotised by the curious three-dimensional triangles on Alec's jumper. 'What do you do as a conservatory consultant?' she asks, and the words rattle around her mouth like barley-sugars.

'I sell greenhouses,' says Alec. His face is pale, insistent.

'I'm just going to top my glass up,' says Rose. 'Excuse me.'

She moves quickly, but not to the drinks table. She makes her way through the crowd, through the kitchen door, closes it very gently, very quietly, and walks upstairs. The carpet on the stairs is clean and white and she looks back to check that she is not leaving muddy marks on it. She has been upstairs in Ellen's house before; she knows the lay-out. There is a bathroom, George and Ellen's room, an unused nursery and a guest room. The guest room is clean and white and simple, as if awaiting a nun or a monk. Ellen knows about interior decoration; she knows that guest rooms should resemble something belonging to a clean goat-herd, uncluttered and wholesome. The bed is covered in a pure cotton bedspread, which has been turned down in a triangle at one corner. There is an oak chest of drawers under the window, a chair, a bowl of pot pourri and two or three books about ministers and the local countryside. Rose has no reason for coming upstairs; she will just have to go into the bathroom, wash her hands and go back down again. But there is the temptation to open the guest room door, to walk in and lie on the bed, gazing at the sky through the window until the party is over. She puts her hand out and pushes the door. George is in there. 'Oh,' says Rose, 'Sorry.' George is sitting on the bed with a goldfish bowl in his arms.

'Please come in,' says George.

'Well, I was just going downstairs,' says Rose.

'So why did you open the door?' says George. 'You were going to nose around, weren't you?' There is a little rise in his voice, a lilt that makes her feel cold. He looks at the goldfish. 'I just rescued them,' he says. 'The music was disturbing them.'

Rose wonders if he is cracking up. She would certainly crack up if she was married to Ellen. She sits down on a small oak chair.

'I hate everyone here except you,' says George.

'Oh,' says Rose. 'That's nice.'

'Do you like goldfish?' says George.

'Not particularly,' says Rose. 'I prefer cats.'

'That's what I like about you,' says George. 'You don't lie.'

'I lie all the time actually,' says Rose.

'How can I tell?' George smiles. His smile is on one side of his face. 'No, but,' he says, 'how's work?'

'I am working on an A to Z of phobias at the moment.'

'Is there an Ellen – a – phobia?' he asks, and she realises, suddenly, that he is drunk. He has probably drunk most of a bottle of wine. His mouth is stained a dark red.

'Ellen is afraid no-one likes her,' he says. 'It's probably true.'

'I don't think that's very kind,' she says. She can hear Ellen laughing downstairs, a loud, open-mouthed laugh. She'll be in the kitchen, standing there in her yellow dress with her head thrown back just the right distance, with just the right amount of wine in her glass.

George lifts the goldfish bowl up and stares into it. His face is as round as a stone. 'Ellen thinks you are her best friend,' he says.

'I'm going downstairs now,' says Rose.

'Yes,' says George, suddenly loud. 'Go, before I seduce you.'

He doesn't move. He stays on the bed, cradling the goldfish bowl. His eyes are bloodshot.

'Seduce,' says Rose, 'not seduct,' but he doesn't answer.

Walking downstairs she thinks of her husband, fishing in a deep, black lake, one holiday.

'Rose,' says Ellen, when she returns to the kitchen. She stops a conversation abruptly with a man who was telling her about golfing tees. She propels Rose into the hallway, faces her and smiles. When a party is going well, when her friends are having a good time, her eyes are a deep, sad blue. 'Rose,' she says, in her cathedral voice, 'how are you coping?' and she moves close and looks into her eyes. She never forgets that Rose carries this ghost around with her, this emptiness. 'Are you OK?' she says. 'Shall we go and have a little chat somewhere quiet?'

'I'm all right,' says Rose. 'I'll be going soon,' but she puts her arms around Ellen for a while and leans her head on her big, perfumed shoulder.

'You are a good friend,' she says.

Strange Birds

M Y DOWNSTAIRS NEIGHBOUR Mrs Kington owns a canary. I can hear it now at three in the morning clattering against metal. Its cage stands directly beneath me on Mrs Kington's washing machine, and the bird flies from bell to cuttle-fish all night. Mrs Kington's cat gazes at it with beautiful eyes, as if it's not really thinking of birdslaughter.

There are all kinds of noises at this time in the morning. From the flat next door comes the sound of sheets rustling, bed springs, washed feet catching the bedclothes. Upstairs someone flushes the lavatory. A door closes. Keys. And the fridge makes a racket. It always seems to make more noise after midnight as if it is lonely and humming to itself.

During the day Mrs Kington sits on the ledge outside the front door and watches people. She always wears a PVC coat. Sometimes I stop for a bit and we talk about the weather or Christmas/Easter/summer holidays. She has relations in Bournemouth, she tells me, but she doesn't visit them. She also has a friend called Reeny who she does visit. They sit and smoke and eat cakes and Reeny's budgie screeches, 'Hallo, Reen,' every few minutes. 'I'm glad my canary doesn't talk,' Mrs Kington told me. 'It would drive me nuts.'

I kick the edge of the curtain with my toe. The curtain is thick at the edges and thin in the middle, like an old sheet. Maybe it's to do with the sunlight. It still looks dark outside but there is something about the sky that looks as if dawn is imminent. A blackbird sings, and someone taps down the unlit pavement on high heels. Late party. Or maybe another breakfast waitress. At 4.45 I get up. There is no point trying to sleep now. I blunder in the cold greyness and switch lights on.

Across the stairway Mr Heinemann is whistling. He appears sometimes on the stairs in stripey pyjama trousers and it makes me wonder if anyone sleeps. I am surrounded by sleepless people. In the kitchen I switch on the television, which is just revving up for the day – a still picture of a tree and some tragic music. I sit in front of it and drink tea, half-expecting the tree to move. At five o'clock, a man's voice says Good Morning this is BBC2. A world revolves on the screen. By now I have caught up with my usual routine. Five am and it almost feels late. I finish my tea quickly and begin to get jittery. I have to be in position at the Cumberland by six. I work the revolving toast rack. Mrs Kington is always looking out for better jobs for me. She buys the *Evening News* and circles adverts she thinks will interest me. The jobs are usually things connected with galleries or bookshops because she tells me I am artistic; it is because of my earrings. I have parrot earrings and she laughs at them and says they're almost as big as her canary.

'Have you got names for them?' she asked one morning. Her canary is called Charlie.

Now my parrots wait to adorn my ears, sitting on the fridge. Guests at the Cumberland look at them strangely, these green birds swinging at them as I pour coffee. They don't go with the uniform. But I suppose when you are sitting in a two-star hotel at six in the morning eating tinned grapefruit segments, most things seem strange. The early eaters sit pale and remote like quiet children while waitresses shush about the carpet with fried eggs and anaemic porridge. It is an enveloping experience, a little removed from the rest of the day when they will plunge into the tweedy shops or onto the heather. Evening waitresses tell me that the guests are more boisterous. They tell jokes and laugh loud, strengthened by weather and whisky.

I open the flat door and lock it behind me. This is the fourth floor and there is a small tree outside Mr Heinemann's door. A token effort to cheer the landing up. Before I can get down the stairs, Mr Heinemann opens his door and stands in his pyjama trousers, pulling leaves off the tree.

'Couldn't sleep,' he says, 'what with the noise.'

I proceed to the third floor. Mr Heinemann shouts over the balcony, 'Off to your waitress job, are you?'

'Afraid so.'

I didn't know he knew about my waitressing job. Maybe Mrs Kington told him. When I walk across the third-floor landing there is nothing outside Mrs Kington's door apart from a fake grass doormat.

The revolving toast rack is called 'The Elite.' You put six slices of bread on each surface, and it revolves like a spit and after a while the toast burns and you have to start again. The worst thing is when people request Melba toast. Then you have to cut slices of bread in half down the thickness of it and it is meant to end up crisp and golden but it burns even easier. Little smoking holes as if someone has stubbed out cigarettes against them. And you can't butter them. They collapse into brittle crumbs.

The breakfast staff get no early morning bonus. Only desperate people have jobs like this, so the Cumberland pays peanuts. My work has no impact on my debts. But there is a good side to the job; breakfast waitressing happens so early that it's probably *not* happening: we pour coffee in our sleep and are away again by 9.45.

This morning there is the elderly American group with elasticated trousers; two businessmen trying to butter Melba toast significantly; one young family requesting a high chair; and the Resident, who gets smiles, more marmalade in his pot and first read of the *Independent*. Others shuffle in and out. Some stand vacantly at the buffet, peering with mild horror at the black pudding and kedgeree. There is a steel cauldron of simmering oil that the waitresses break eggs into. The eggs cook in a few seconds and get whisked out, shimmering, with a ladle. If it is your turn to stand at the buffet, you have to have your hands behind your back unless you are serving, God knows why. Maybe it's a sin to reveal your hands when they're not wiping down some table or rearranging sausages. I try to avoid the buffet; I prefer going into a trance at the toast rack, nudging blackening slices off the hot plate and letting them fall into a big basket. Anyway I am useless at balance; I've got the kind of ankles that buckle. Yesterday I dropped half a melon on a man's lap. Everything seemed to slow down for a minute, like a freeze-frame with this big pink-faced man in it, gazing at this green thing with cherries on his lap. I gazed at it too; so did everyone else in the breakfast room, then time bounced back and the man laughed and said, 'Novel codpiece.' He is still here, but I notice he sits in the corner of the room and averts his eyes when I ramble past.

The Resident is already slathering his toast with marmalade when I make my appearance. He looks up and cackles at me, dropping gunge on the front page of the newspaper.

'Where are your danglies today, my love?' he says and I wonder what he's talking about then I put my hands up to my ears and realise I'm not wearing the parrot earrings. I left them on the fridge. The Resident is from Essex but has lived here for six years. He says he wouldn't go back now, he'd miss all his lovely ladies. I say something vague and take a quick look at the headlines. MINISTER IN LOVE TRIANGLE.

Standing at the toast rack, there is more news about the junior minister and his personal assistant, a lot of voices on the breakfast show, and jokes. The minister was a LAY PREACHER. The woman was his PERSONAL assistant. Enough said, said the radio presenter. The other waitresses, Mandy and Sarah and Chris, talk about it with a kind of bleary interest. None of us really knows each other, we're all part of a collective dream. You forget conversations as soon as you walk out of the door. But I'm beginning to wake up a bit now, feeling better – and there's no bad news on the radio about America. My brother has just gone away to America and I'm always sad about people leaving,

145

especially my brother. My brother seems short and vulnerable, my wee brother. I'm thinking about him sitting in a yellow cab speeding across Bay Bridge in the sun when someone says, 'Phone call for you, hen.' No-one ever phones me here, no-one's awake to phone me, so my heart flips a bit and I drop the toast and walk to the phone.

'Hallo?' I croak and clear my throat.

'Hallo?' says a voice. A woman's voice. It doesn't reassure me.

'Hallo,' I say.

'This is Mrs Kington.'

I stare at the fire extinguisher on the wall which says Strike Nozzle Here, and can't think what to say. I can't think why Mrs Kington is phoning me.

Mrs Kington says, 'OK to phone you at work, is it?'

'Yes, it's fine but I have to get back to the toast in a second.'

Mrs Kington seems reluctant to tell me why she's phoning but after a pause she asks me what time I finish work.

'9.45.'

'Well,' says Mrs Kington, 'I'll be in the West End at nine because I've got a dentist's appointment so I thought maybe I'd drop by and we could have a coffee after you've clocked off.'

I wonder what would happen if I struck the nozzle of the fire extinguisher.

'That's fine, that's fine,' I say. 'Come into the breakfast room at 10 and we'll have a coffee. Nothing wrong, is there?'

'No,' says Mrs Kington but she sounds doubtful. I can hear her canary twittering in the background. 'See you later then,' says Mrs Kington and she hangs up.

When I walk back into the breakfast room, the Resident is leaving for the day. Someone else is clearing his table.

'Don't forget the birds tomorrow,' he says, and he creaks through the door.

I suppose if you can afford it it's not bad to get your bed made every day, your cooking done. Just that it might get lonely, this hotel room at night with the grey walls and the pink curtain and the picture of a Victorian sweetie-pie on the wall, fluttering eyelashes. Not home. Although he has residential concessions. Electrical ones to make life more familiar. A kettle, a TV, an electric blanket. I don't think he goes far during the day. I saw him once sitting on a bench, feeding a squirrel and he waved at me across the traffic. He likes it here, he says. You don't need to go far to find wildlife. In Chelmsford, he said, everything was too neat. Even the pavements; they looked washed.

My brother might be looking at the bison now in Golden Gate Park. He told me there is a pub he wants to go to called the Edinburgh Castle. 'I'll check it out,' he said, speaking American before he'd even got there. But maybe, he said, the whisky would be ridiculously expensive and no-one would really be Scottish, they would just think they were. They would maybe slap him on the back and talk about Loch Ness.

I spend the hour between 9 and 10 shaking crumbs from the revolving toast rack. Mandy and Sarah and Chris are talking about Chris's new perm.

'I said I wanted a root perm, just for a bit of lift,' says Chris. Her hair stands half a foot above her head, in tight ringlets.

'It'll die down,' says Mandy.

When I go to get the egg cauldron, Mrs Kington is there. She is sitting at one of the tables in her PVC coat. She has a shopping bag from Harrods that says 50% cotton, 50% PVC. She is a shining, waving woman in the centre of the room.

'With you in a minute,' I shout, and I wheel away with the egg cauldron.

'Is that your mum?' says Mandy. She is touching up her lipstick, looking in the square mirror next to the coat rack.

'Just an old friend,' I say.

'Oh' says Mandy, and she smiles, staring at someone else in the mirror.

Everyone seems puzzled about this woman dressed in PVC in the Breakfast Suite. I wonder what we are going to talk

147

about. Chris and Sarah and Mandy leave. 'See you tomorrow,' I tell them. I say this every day. Chris has broken down again because of her hair and Sarah is saying, 'Get some conditioner. It'll be much better if you put conditioner on it. Honest. Or some hot oil.'

The door bangs and it is silent. I take out two cups of coffee and sit with Mrs Kington. She is chewing a toffee. We talk about the rain for a while, which is slopping past the window, and we talk about her dentist appointment. 'Two fillings,' she says, and her jaws unclench suddenly because they were stuck against the toffee. She unbelts her coat and it makes me think of wipe-clean table cloths. Mrs Kington sighs and stirs sugar into her coffee. She says, 'Can you look after my canary, for me?'

I swig coffee. 'Your canary,' I say.

'My cat nearly got him last night,' she says.

I nod as if I knew this already, but I suppose it was obvious really, the cat probably having tried it every night the bird's been there.

'Can't Reeny have it?' I say.

This seems like a good idea to me, but Mrs Kington says Reeny's budgie would get jealous.

'I'll pay you,' she says. 'Millet plus a bit extra.'

'I'd rather have the cat,' I tell her.

'Oh,' she says, 'but I'd rather let go of Charlie than Percy.'

I think of the yellow canary that I've never seen, just heard. Scraping its beak against the cuttlefish. Tapping the bell.

'Can you really not take him?'

Mrs Kington's coat creases when she moves her hands up to her face. It goes into a hundred shiny creases.

I never thought I'd see anything of the Cumberland apart from the Breakfast Suite and here I am smuggling canaries up to the Resident's room. The Resident is sure the hotel won't mind. He talks very fast when he is excited. As we go upstairs, he is talking about my parrot earrings again, which I remembered to put on this morning, and the wildlife in Essex and an old pekinese his mother used to have when he was a boy. He says all this in a high and cracking voice. He also talks to Charlie, whose cage is wobbling in his hands.

When we get to his room, he attaches Charlie's cage to the stand and takes the plastic hood off. Charlie looks very yellow against the greyish walls.

'Nice view he's got,' says the Resident. 'Level with the tree tops.'

I think this must be the worst view for a caged bird, but I don't say anything.

'Nice to have my own bit of wildlife,' says the Resident. He stands and clutches Mrs Kington's phone number. It is strange to have introduced him to Mrs Kington, to have connected them. The reason for the introduction flits about like a smudge of yellow paint. It is whistling the melody line of 'Sailing By.'

'I didn't know he could do that,' I say. The canary is singing the high notes, the tuneful bit. I'm just used to the base, through Mrs Kington's ceiling.

'Clever boy, aren't you?' says the Resident. He is delighted. He scoops up a handful of millet and pours it in Charlie's tray.

Sitting on the ledge in her PVC coat, Mrs Kington chews sweets and never mentions Charlie to me. The Resident has breakfast in his room these days, and I never see him. I scrape toast and miss him. I miss his comments about my earrings. I got a postcard from my brother the other day; he talks about yellow cabs and it makes me think of canaries. I still listen to the thuds of 'Sailing By' on Mrs Kington's radio and wonder if she is as lonely as me. It's strange: the absence of a canary makes a big difference to sleepless hours. Mr Heinemann is the only one who still whistles, tunelessly, in his pyjamas.

The Doggies

THIS WAS IN a city full of stray dogs. They curled up in parks and beside flower stalls as if they were in their own gardens. Sometimes if you had your head in the air you might trip over one, hiding behind the freesias.

As well as dogs there was graffiti, making buildings look dispossessed, like something out of a film called *Wilderness* or *The Deserted Planet*. There were also posters of politicians fighting it out at bus stops. People would rip these posters down and there would be older ones peering through, underneath. Pictures of men with beards and brown suits and expressions: they tried so hard to have that look of integrity but somehow they always failed. They just looked frightening, smiling over the fields on the outskirts of the city, accosting people in supermarkets and outside cinemas. There were broken pavements, and rain would get underneath the paving stones. If you trod on the wrong slab it would flip up and you would be covered in black water. Sometimes the pavements floated away completely.

John O'Keefe lived in this city. It got to him occasionally. He had to get out, even if it meant just wandering past the billboards in the fields, to be able to turn and look back. He didn't feel so owned by them if he couldn't see them. He worked as a dog-walker. People in this city owned a lot of pedigrees; it was a strange fact that it you were long-haired and difficult to look after your future was secure. Some Saturdays he walked through the rich part of town looking for new customers. He had to do this every so often because his dogs had a habit of moving away or injuring themselves, as pedigrees do.

At the bottom of a flight of long white stairs a greying woman with matching eyeshadow examined one of his cards. He felt embarrassed about the spirals he had used as decoration.

'Professional dog-walker?' she said. 'I didn't know there was such a thing.'

'There sure is,' said John, putting that snappy old smile in his voice that he had learned about on a 'selling skills' course for the unemployed.

'Do you walk them individually or in groups?'

'Both. Individual is a little extra an hour.'

'Well, this is ideal,' said the woman, exaggerating with her lipsticked mouth and assessing him with her shadowed eyes. 'I have three alsatians that need loads of walks. Come.'

She led him up the white stairs. He had to pause behind her floral-printed plodding because she was slow and they kept nearly being on the same step.

'This is a very impressive flat,' said John. The steps disappeared into a space of wooden floorboards and clean windows and potted plants. There were parrots, wooden ones, hanging from the boughs of umbrella plants and the place smelled of honey and biscuits.

'Thank you,' said the woman. 'My husband is an interior designer.'

Then she trod brittly across the floorboards and shouted, 'Doggies.'

The doggies appeared from a small room that had a lot of washing machinery in it. They looked like wolves. John resisted an impulse to run as they lurked by his feet. They had the amber eyes of wolves, full of colour and somehow sightless.

'This is Ivan,' said the woman. 'This is Boris. And this is Rostropovich.'

'Interesting names,' said John. The alsatians flopped their tongues out and panted.

'Here are their leads. Shall we say an hour a day, Monday to

151

Friday? My husband and I will walk them at weekends or we'll never get to see you, will we, babies?' She pouted at them. The dogs stared back with their mad scary eyes.

'I can give you references,' said John, wondering where these words came from sometimes, that landed in his mouth.

'I don't think we'll need references. The doggies can take care of themselves.'

The next day he put on heavy, anti-molesting clothes. A creaking jacket. Big boots through which he wouldn't feel collapsing pavements or sideways lunges at his ankle. He walked to the woman's house and picked up the alsatians. He attached collars to leads and set off for the municipal park. On the way he met other dog-walkers and felt a sense of belonging, the way taxi-drivers wave to each other and seem to have a secret language about their passengers. His doggies were better-behaved when the woman wasn't there giving them chocolate biscuits. They trotted very quietly and he thought about attaching a sledge and coasting through the park in winter shouting 'Mush, mush!' Their fur was dense and silver.

They had walked about twenty minutes when they reached the park. He let them loose and stood under a eucalyptus tree with the proud symbol of professional dog-walkers, a bunch of leads, dangling from his hands. The dogs ran around the park, knocking the swings with their tails and making dustclouds. The swings were vandalised with words, and the trees had been stabbed with penknives, had had bark ripped off the trunks. The dogs had to pick their feet up high so they didn't trip over chasms in the ground. It made them look proud and slightly appalled. A lot of the city's strays used the park: there were dozens of them, curled up like sacks under the trees but the alsatians ignored them. Individuals against the flea-ridden populace.

It is curious how stray dogs stay together in lonely packs. Even when they sleep they choose the same patch of ground to lie in and sometimes they move in their dreams, ripping the dry yellow grass with long claws, turning and showing how thin and pink the skin is under the fur. All medium-sized muts, which is why they are strays – toy poodles would not last the night. Most of these have a particular look; grey wilting faces like satchels. They do not beg any more; they have given up trying to look pretty. The alsatians barged round like mobile sofas. That swaying prance that well-fed dogs have, sniffing everything as if they might be tested on it later. A pale mongrel was watching, lying underneath a silver birch tree, and now it flopped upright and lurched towards John. It was grey and probably white if it had a bath. John wondered how long these animals lasted. Six months? Four years? He wasn't sure about stray dog survival rates. Everywhere he went there were dogs asleep or scratching fleas from their loose skin, as common and infested as pigeons. Sometimes he might kick over a bone that someone had chucked onto the street for them but at night the dogs howled because they were hungry and barked monotonously in the cold air as if they were trying to get his attention before the day finished. It was easy to forget about strays because they ended up relying on themselves, tipping up the contents of rubbish bins, sleeping in doorways and by warm air vents. He had seen some organising games for themselves, standing at traffic lights and snapping at car wheels, then running back and doing it again at the next green light. It made him think of shepherding. Motorcyclists were particularly good targets: lone stupid sheep. The grey-white dog wagged its tail and gave him a dog-smile.

Two children in green plastic sacks with armholes were fighting over a tyre that hung from a tree. One of them was saying, 'It's mine, it's mine,' and the other was singing, 'You're a big-fat cow-ow.' John whistled to the alsatians because he had to leave. He had to leave. They walked back past all the same posters that said, 'We're Improving The City For You.' Someone had torn a triangle out of one and you could see the eye, just the eye, of an earlier politician blinking through. Like a cyclops.

John's parents came to visit that weekend because it was his birthday. They bought him a big cake with sliced almonds instead of candles. He felt too old but touched.

'Oh,' said his mother. 'Isn't that a sweet dog? What's his name?'

'Where?' said John.

'Down there in the backyard.'

He looked out of the window and saw the grey dog, doing a kind of balancing act on the fence by the rubbish bins.

'Is he a stray?'

'He's been following me about a bit recently.'

'I see.' His father straightened up a tea-towel that was hanging over the ironing board, and looked at his wife.

'Big responsibility, a dog,' he said. 'Remember Snitch? He got through two tins of dogfood a day.'

Snitch was an Irish wolfhound that used to pull John around on a sledge during the winter.

'He died in '76, didn't he?' said his mother, 'Or was it '77?'

'It was '76,' said his father, squashing together a little mountain of cake crumbs and putting it in his mouth, 'because it was the same year that Edna died.'

'Was it? Are you sure?'

Whenever they came to see him, his parents had disagreements about dates. It seemed important, to fix things down like that.

Halfway through the afternoon it started raining. Water that had been lying in wait beneath the ceiling plaster began to well out. John tried to push his parents out of the kitchen but the splashes were too quick and the big, dependable one started dripping into the sink.

'You really should get your ceiling replastered,' said his mother.

'You should poke a hole in the plaster,' said his father. 'Relieves the tension on the weak parts.'

John's flat normally had some kind of smell in it related to stale water. It could be bad plumbing in the kitchen or the cabbagy musk of the thin carpet by the window which always leaked. Before his parents came he would run around the flat with a bottle of disinfectant, trying to eliminate odours. It covered things for a couple of hours and his mother always said, 'Your flat has such a clean smell,' when she walked through the door. It made him feel guilty.

154

When there was only a small triangle of cake left he began to detect the return of the plumbing smell. Faint but there. Before his parents noticed he suggested they went for a walk in the park, in the rain. He had forgotten that it was not the kind of place he should take them. The dog followed. 'This is where I bring the alsatians,' said John, feeling like a tour guide, sweeping grandly past the puddled playground.

'I've never liked alsatians much,' said his mother. 'Unpredictable things.' Then she said, 'I think it's got worse here since we last came.' The dog kept a discreet distance, dodging behind the trees.

When he got to the underground the next day, the dog was sitting by the newspaper stall. A man was throwing bits of rolled-up paper at it, and it would lope away for a minute and then come back again. John bought a paper and it had an advert on the front page – one of the men in brown suits. 'Together We Can Make It Better' said the slogan, and the man had a large bendy-looking nose and brown dots for eyes. They knew something was bad, then, or they wouldn't say they could make it better. John turned the page and there was another one, except it was a happy blonde child this time gazing at a flower and the slogan was 'A Future For Us All.' Who thought these things up? Who said 'A Future For Us All'?

On the train the safety-handles hung like plastic fruit and swung crazily around all the corners. No-one was holding onto them, but just propped themselves up against the walls. The safety-handles seemed to have a life of their own; the way they swung. John watched them all the way to the centre, as an alternative to reading the walls. This carriage had been taken up by an advert for Private Health Schemes. One stop before he got off, an old man with a gritty voice crept through the door with a box of oven lighters dangling from a piece of string round his neck. 'Bargain lighters,' he was yelling, clicking one in each hand as if they were revolvers. People suddenly got very interested in the Private Health Scheme advert. The man stood near John and clicked the lighters at selected passengers. A girl cowered as if the blue sparks might really hurt her. The man got off at the same stop as John and sagged madly away, down the platform.

This is what happened for a month or more. Every weekday he got the underground to the woman's house. With different dogs to walk, he always developed different routines, had different journeys to make. And with dogs moving away or injuring themselves, he had on average four new routines every year. Once when he was very young he had thought he would have a permanent job: some career in the centre of the city with a sloping desk and vending machines. He would spring out of his white-pillowed bed and arrive early wearing a shirt and tie. It amazed him now, to think that he could have been so idealistic.

The woman liked him to arrive efficiently before breakfast. When he returned with the alsatians already fresh and walked at 8.30, she would be on her second cup of coffee, sitting at the kitchen table and wearing a man's initialled dressing gown. John never saw the husband. He wondered if he was already at a sloping desk in the city somewhere, or lurking in the bedroom. But he must have been at work because after a few weeks the woman began to get flirty with him, calling him 'a mere boy,' 'a baby' and touching him unnecessarily to get to the kettle. Most days she made him a cup of tea. Sometimes, to escape, he would pretend he had an important meeting to attend. She never looked as if she believed him. One morning she said, 'Is that your dog that comes with you most days?'

'Well it's kind of attached itself to me. It's a stray.'

'Oh,' said the woman and she poured herself a little torrent of hot coffee from the jug. A few of the wooden parrots seemed to have flown into the kitchen and were now balanced on top of work-units. There were several primary coloured tea-pots standing on the window sill, and the bin was hidden inside a cupboard. She swung the door open to throw his tea-bag in there.

'Sad, isn't it,' she said, 'but they are a menace.'

She patted one of the alsatians on the head. John could never remember which was which. It was lying over her slippered feet, panting and smelling stale. The whole kitchen smelled of wet fur. 'One of the best things they could do would be to clear the strays up,' she said. 'Humanely,' she added. 'I'm sure that would win a lot of votes.'

She smiled, as if she expected him to say something. Then she looked away as shyly as possible, like a girl. John could see her polished toe-nails, just visible beneath the alsation's fur. He tried to swallow too much hot Darjeeling and burned his lip against the mug. It was difficult to drink out of anyway, being shaped like an elephant, one ear acting as the handle. There was so much jungle stuff in this place. The woman touched his shoulder with her fingernails to get to the window. She opened it and shouted, 'Go away doggy. John doesn't want you.'

Then she giggled and sat down rather sharply.

'A quick humane injection,' she said. 'That would be a start.'

'I must get going,' said John standing up and knocking his head against one of the free-swinging parrots. 'I have to meet someone at 10.' He ran down the steps and met the dog in the alley-way to her garden. It was a very silent dog. It never barked.

When they got back he found an end of salami in the fridge and let the dog eat it in the backyard. He hoped it liked pepperami. He had a strange anger that settled on days when nothing worked and the pavements squirted him with black water like octopuses. It made him want to howl. He picked up the phone and left a message with his landlord.

'The kitchen ceiling is leaking badly. Please send a plumber.'

He went into the bedroom where he stood by the window, creaking the linen basket against the glass with his stomach. The dog was scratching itself in the yard with its head in the air. Little grey hairs were flying everywhere. The dog suited the place – mangey and sadly optimistic. It trotted around the washing pole and sniffed the drain-cover, as if it was debating whether to move in. Then it looked up. The sky didn't look as if it should be above the city; it looked more like a sea sky, striped blue and white, fast-moving and bright. The dog got to work again with its scratching leg and panted. John glazed his eyes and his mouth made a little groaning noise. Life was never the way it should be.

He phoned his mother.

'John,' she said. 'Can you call back? Your father needs me to help saw a branch off the tree.'

'OK,' said John. He knew which tree it was: a beech. Beautiful but much too big, standing in the little square of garden in front of their living room window. It took away most of the light.

'We're improving the quality of our lives,' said his mother. She said things like that. When it rained the leaves blocked the overflow. He imagined his parents standing in the wet grass with a saw and an old table-cloth to catch the branch.

He put the kettle on in the kitchen and peeled away a little of the ceiling paper. There was a stain spreading like green blood. In the bedroom the walls were sad with thin shadows and dust. Posters were peeling off them, revealing blu-tack, old and calcified. He had read an article recently that said most of the young anarchists were respectable people these days, working in the city.

At 11.06 he phoned the woman.

'Is it possible to come any earlier to walk the dogs?' said John. 'This person I met this morning wants me to do some work for them that starts at 9.00 and I . . . I . . .'

His lie was creeping guiltily like a slow-moving mammal. The woman did not interrupt. There was a chasm at the other end of the line.

'And I just wondered if it might be possible to . . .'

'I see,' said the woman. There was a scary glint in her voice. Sharp and manicured.

'Do you still want this job, John?' she said. 'Because there are plenty of young men who would like it.' Now she had a chickeny sort of cluck. She was forgiving him already now she had power. 'Why don't we talk about this tomorrow?' she said. 'Stay for tea and we can talk about it properly, work out what suits.'

'That would be fine,' said John. This was not what he had

envisaged. Another cup of Darjeeling. 'Goodbye,' he said, as light-heartedly as he could manage. 'See you tomorrow then.'

'7.30 sharp,' giggled the woman.

'Ha ha ha,' said John. He put the phone down. He could hear plaster cracking in the kitchen.

At a bus-stop on the way to the vet's, a man was taking down a brown-suit poster and replacing it with one sponsored by the Methodist Society. A big white cross and a rainbow. 'There Is Hope' it said. On the other side of the street the corresponding bus-stop had one that said, 'You Are Never Defeated With Jesus.'

The vet's was full of cardboard boxes. A woman in a coat that looked like soggy leaves poked her finger through an airhole in the top of one box. 'Oo-oo,' she said to its occupant. 'Oo-oo.' On the other side of the room a small red setter flipped about, winding its lead around metal chair legs. 'You can tell who's the youngest in the room,' said the woman with the leaf coat, and she made a small, crackly laugh. John sat very still with the dog. Next to John was a boy with a Cheesy Wotsits box.

'Is that a cat you've got there?' John enquired, feeling kind, mature.

'No, it's a snake,' said the boy. He had a green turtle-neck jumper on that made him look a little reptilian himself.

'Oh,' said John, and he patted the dog's cool back.

'O'Keefe,' said a woman with beige shoes, walking into the room. John stood up and dragged the dog into the surgery. A sign on the door said, 'Have you had your pet wormed?' The room was very hot with a smell that might be fear.

'So this dog is a stray,' said the vet. Her coat was ironed stiff like a tablecloth. There was some bladed instrument in her top pocket.

'Yes. I found him in the park.'

'A dog is a big responsibility,' she said, 'People don't realise this.' And she sighed for a long time. Then she directed her voice towards the dog. 'Right then, Doggo,' she said, 'let's jump up here.' She preferred talking to Doggo. Doggo lay on the white examining table, smiling as if he was remembering jokes. There

159

was animal hair pushed to the side of the table, and the floor was covered in a kind of sludge that could have been disinfectant. On the wall there was a cartoon picture of a blue cat which had a bubble coming out of its mouth. 'Feline Leukaemia?' it said. 'It doesn't worry me now.' Then there were all sorts of smaller, more worrying sentences underneath.

'You're in good shape for a stray,' said the vet, pulling the dog's left ear around its head and leaving it flopped over the top like a pink hairband. 'Fleas,' she said to John 'And worms, of course.'

'Of course,' said John.

Her sentences speeded up as if she did not want to be answered. He did not know what to say anyway. On his way out, he bought a red collar and a lead at Dispensaries, and a small orange ball that squeaked occasionally and had a badly formed face on it. 'Lucky dog,' said the leaf-coat woman. And her cardboard box made a little scrabbly noise.

Sea Monster Tattoo

S OMETIMES, IF YOU lean against walls, men pull up in cars. 'Eh,' they say, 'show you good time, honey.' Yesterday there were four of them, waving their arms out of the windows, like tarantulas in T-shirts. But it's OK because Hazel knows the art of self-defence. She knows all the right body-swerves.

We are waiting for a ferry now. It is two in the morning and we are standing next to a lorry full of sheep. Lucy looks at the ground and says, 'Maybe we should have got a coffee in that place.'

'What,' says Hazel, 'in the Greasy Spoon?'

'It wasn't a greasy spoon,' says Lucy.

'It was full of sailors,' says Hazel.

The boat on the horizon has lights in it. Pretty. Some of the men shout and light up acrid cigarettes. A short man who seems to have joined us says, 'It is here in ten minutes.' He stands very close and has a tattoo on his arm.

'Are we in the right queue?' I say.

'There isn't a queue,' says Hazel.

The sheep in the lorry are silent. I can just see bums and yellow eyes.

It is June but the air trickles against my skin like cold water. The short man grabs my arm and pinches it between thick fingers, hard enough to give me a thumb-shaped bruise.

'Quick,' he says, and he pushes me towards the edge of the quay. The ferry is so close now it's just a piece of cast iron, near

161

enough for us to feel the noise of engines through the tarmac. The man has pushed me in the right direction, because I am first up the gangplank, and when I get on deck more people press their thumbs against my arms, their hands against my back. The ferry floor is painted green and it's so hard it almost hurts to walk on it. Everything is bolted together like civic furniture. After about ten minutes I meet Lucy and Hazel on the deck, next to the funnel. Hazel says we ought to commandeer some seats in the lounge. She uses that word: commandeer. Maybe it is because we are on a ferry. Hazel's rucksack has straps in the right place, useful compartments and a proper frame. My rucksack slouches on my back like an overweight toddler. The zip on Lucy's rucksack has broken and she has put half her stuff in a canvas bag that she bought in Venice. The bag has pictures of carnival faces on it; happy and sad. I stare at them as we slither up a staircase.

Inside the ferry we take a wrong turning because none of us speaks Italian. We walk down a wooden staircase and along passageways, then stop at a door that says DANGER, in English. We do not open it; the sea is behind it. We retrace our steps, Lucy and I following Hazel's framed rucksack in silence. When we get to the lounge all the chairs are occupied by people with more rucksacks, and we recognise some Scandinavians we met on a train. They all have their eyes closed. One of them is resting his feet in huge trainers on an empty seat and Lucy says, 'Bloody selfish,' but none of us wakes them up. The ferry is moving now; the sea slapping against the side. I can see it through a porthole, just a little blacker than the sky. There is nowhere to sit, not even on the floor, so we creep away into the canteen. Someone is playing a piano in the canteen, some rumbling tune which has a lot of repetition in the left hand. The place is full of people talking in Greek and Italian and drinking spirits and there is a smell of aniseed and tar. The short man with the tattoo is standing at the bar, picking at a loose piece of formica with his little finger. The formica is supposed to look like wood, but it doesn't.

'Right,' says Hazel. She pushes through a cluster of men,

flattening them with her rucksack, and orders three coffees which arrive in glasses. The coffee is milky, not what I expected.

'Cafe Longe. Long coffee,' explains Lucy. No-one replies.

I am hungry but there are just things that look like shredded wheat behind a smeared plastic counter. Hazel says they are Baclava, and she says it really feels like Greece when you see Baclava. 'We're really in Greece now,' she says, even though we have only just left the Italian port. It is the kind of thing my mother used to say.

Lucy says, 'Even more full of Greek sailors in here.'

'What?' says Hazel. She rubs her eyes. Her face is as uncomprehending as uncooked sausage.

Lucy says, 'More in here than in the Greasy Spoon.'

Hazel does not reply. She does not know what Lucy is talking about. The man with the tattoo starts to pick his teeth with a sliver of formica.

'I know a room for you,' he says, and we all ignore him.

It is 2.45 am. I think the crossing takes six hours, but I am no longer reading timetables; to have got this far south seems to be more about luck than timetables.

'Pay me nothing,' says the man.

'It's OK thanks,' says Lucy, turning very slightly away. Her feet shuffle her an inch or so further off.

'Why?' says the man. His voice becomes high and he starts to move his arms around. We have noticed men doing this in Italy. When they are surprised their hands and forearms go out at a forty-five-degree angle and sometimes they make the tips of their fingers into a little beak and then they poke at the air with it.

'Why?' says the man. He taps his head with a hard, wide finger. I can see now what his tattoo is. It is some kind of sea-monster, slightly faded at the edges, like lipstick that has smeared around the corners of a mouth. The sea-monster has a curious smile. Beneath it there is a name but the man moves his arm again before I can read it.

'Why?' says the man.

'For God's sake,' says Hazel.

Out of the corner of my eye I can see the Scandinavian's trainers on the lounge seat. They must be size 14 at least. I hate trainers, the way they are always so huge and white and smelly.

'That Danish bloke's quite dishy, isn't he?' says Lucy.

'I don't go for him myself,' I say.

Lucy has recently split up with her boyfriend. That is why she is here. She was going to go to Turkey with him but he went off with someone else a week beforehand. She had already bought her tickets, and she could, at this very moment, have been standing in a market in Istanbul, buying rugs and flower vases. Her boyfriend was learning Turkish at evening classes, and he always pronounced Istanbul differently from everyone else, as if it was a question about someone called Stan. 'Is Stan Bull?' I don't know what she saw in him but sometimes, in bunk beds and on train seats late at night, I can hear her crying. Hazel tells me she is still in shock and I nod my head. Hazel managed to sell Lucy's tickets for her, and even made her a small profit, which she spent on a book called *Men Are Bastards*.

I am very practical when I talk to Hazel. In Paris we talked about Lucy in quiet voices, buying baguettes and grapes and cheese triangles together at the local supermarket, then, when I went shopping with Lucy the same afternoon we bought jade necklaces and talked about Hazel while she was at the launderette. It makes me feel two-faced. But they talk about me as well so I suppose it's OK. I think they think I am stubborn. Perverse. A word my parents used to use, and which I had never heard again, until now.

The tattoo man says, 'So. I will give other people the room.'

'You do that,' says Hazel. She is so rude; she thinks that if someone is male and from southern Europe they are a fair target. It makes me and Lucy cringe. We usually let it drop but tonight I am tired. I am exhausted. I want to sleep on cotton sheets and have a basin to wash myself in.

I say, 'Come on, Haze,' and my voice sounds like a whimper, pale and desperate.

The tattoo man says, 'Come on, Haze,' and he reveals the palms of his hands, like someone in a Western who isn't carrying a gun.

On our way through the ferry the man opens doors and we trip over small iron lintels.

'What do they put those stupid things there for?' Lucy says. She bends down to rub her shin and her rucksack flops forward, over her shoulder. 'Jesus,' she says. Her eyes look swollen, the way they do when you have been watching a very long, sad film. I wonder what I look like; I haven't seen a mirror for two days. We all have lank hair.

The man is about fifty I suppose, but I'm no good with ages. His hair is still dark but his face has lines. He looks as if he is always thinking up new jokes to tell people.

'You like this boat?' he says to us, over his shoulder.

'It's lovely,' I say.

'It goes up and down, eh?' says the man and he laughs.

I don't reply. The man looks back at me and creases up one of his eyes. I suppose this is a wink but I am too tired to know what to do about it. 'I like it,' he says, 'to go up and down.' I look away and focus on green rivets in the floor. It annoys me that even here, on my way to Greece, I can still let someone's words niggle. The man laughs, turns his back on us and makes up and down movements with his arms. Then he suddenly opens a door and we all trip up into a small cabin. There are two bunk beds on either side of the room. A wooden chair, a basin with a mirror above it, a porthole.

'OK for you?' says the man.

'Free?' says Hazel.

'Of course,' says the man. He sounds surprised. He folds his arms and I can see the sea monster tattoo again, sticking its tongue out.

'OK,' he says abruptly, and he steps over the door lintel. 'You sleep now.'

He leaves behind him a smell of underarm, coarse and sweet as sawdust.

165

Hazel piles our rucksacks and the chair behind the door. She says it is best to be on the safe side. Lucy and I flick glances at each other and it makes me feel good.

After we have been in the cabin for about ten minutes I say, 'We didn't thank him, did we?'

Hazel looks up from the basin. Her head is already covered in mango shampoo.

'So we didn't, she says. The smell of mango is almost overwhelming. She leans forward over the basin again and shouts into the plughole because she thinks we won't hear her. 'He won't mind though,' she says.

We choose bunk beds like six-year-olds. The sheets are cool and clean and wonderful. Hazel pokes about in her rucksack for ages, rustling plastic bags, before she actually gets into bed. Then it is quiet, the three of us lying still, staring at different sections of darkened room. The ferry is quiet now but I don't sleep. I'm thinking of the last time I was on a ferry, in Scotland. It was cold then too, at a strange time in the morning; I had got off some coach, woken up from some strange dream, and I think there were also sheep in a lorry. But I was much younger, travelling with my family. When we got on board there was a fruit machine and decks of cards sticky with beer. The crossing took over four hours. My mother tried to get me to sleep on an orange plastic sofa in the lounge but I just sat and stared out of the window at the sea, which was dark and wide and smooth as chocolate. Lying here, there are cracks in the ceiling that I could touch without even stretching. The light bulb outside our door creates a yellow light, washed out, because there is already dawn seeping through the porthole. After a while I sit up and stare through the porthole. I just watch the sea, a huge wash of grey and think: we could be anywhere in the world.